MAYHEM
AT THE
MUSEUM

MAYHEM AT THE MUSEUM

A NOVEL

REGINA WATTS

 PAINTED BLIND
PUBLISHING
LITERARY ALCHEMY

Mayhem At The Museum
© 2021 Regina Watts
ISBN: 978-1-7363009-8-5

Text: Regina Watts
Typesetting: M. F. Sullivan
Cover: Anton Rosovsky

Regina Watts Online: hrhdegenetrix.com
Painted Blind Publishing: paintedblindpublishing.com
Join Regina's mailing list for three free stories!

BEFORE

THE BRAT WAS finally in bed.

Olivia turned the volume of the television all the way down for the third time to make sure he wasn't still awake. No noises emanated from upstairs. No music played; no toys chimed.

With a sigh of relief, the babysitter muted the television altogether and took her opportunity to call Leroy.

"Hey," he said without formal greeting, "I was just thinking about you."

"Shut up." Olivia laughed and, at his protest, ("It's true!"), she settled back into the arm of the Watsons' couch and cradled the device in her shoulder. With her free hand propping up her head, she said, "Sure. Well, don't tell me *what* you were thinking...I don't want to know, especially if I'm not there with you."

"You workin' tonight, babe?"

"Sure am."

"Man! When are you gonna *quit* that gig and get a real job? Someplace I can come hang out with you, like a late shift at a restaurant or something."

"And lose this free study time? No, thanks."

Upstairs, a floorboard creaked. The house settling? She had to hope...the Watson kid was a real pain sometimes, always getting up and down and getting into mischief.

Then, of course, there was the house.

While her boyfriend called her a nerd, she said, "Tell that to my transcript, jerk... Anyway, I don't know. I hate the idea of waiting tables."

"Couldn't be worse than having to deal with that kid."

"Come on! He's not so bad. You don't even *know* him."

"You only talk about him to complain."

Twisting an auburn strand of hair around her finger, Olivia glanced toward the flashing light and color of the television.

"Doesn't everybody complain about their job? Luther's not even the problem, really."

"What is it?"

Olivia didn't like to think about it too much. Suddenly aware that she had let the living room grow dim with the falling of night, she slid over to turn on the lamp beside the couch.

"I don't know," she lied. "It's always just a little

spooky to be in somebody else's house by yourself all night, watching after a kid."

"'The call is coming from inside the house,'" her boyfriend said in an obnoxiously spooky voice that made her roll her eyes.

"If you were here, Leroy, I'd punch you."

Silence held the line for about three seconds. "Do you *want* me to be there?"

"I mean..."

Olivia looked at the clock, her top row of teeth running back and forth over her worrying lip. It was tempting...but Mr. and Mrs. Watson would be home in another two hours. Three, at the absolute most. She could get a lot of work done in that time, and that idea was just too attractive to ignore.

"I've watched this kid so many times before, Leroy...I'm fine, really."

"Suit yourself," he said with a slightly put-upon tone. "Guess I'll catch you tomorrow, babe."

"Hey, don't—"

The dickhead hung up on her.

Well, damn! This was the last time she dated an athlete...sorry she didn't have time or liberty to stroke your ego, dude. It was somebody *else's* house, after all.

Wondering how she was going to have the conversation of "I'm over this" with him, Olivia set her phone down and scooped up her books. After pushing a few strands of hair from her eyes, she leaned back in the couch to crack open her German textbook.

The flickering of the television halted her, catching her eye and reeling it back in before she could even start a sentence. Comforting, but distracting. With the heavy book open in her lap, Olivia plucked up the remote and shut the television off.

Something moved in the screen's dark reflection of the stairs.

Startled, Olivia whipped her head toward the real stairwell in time to see the tip of something—a black robe, maybe, or more likely a cape with this kid—vanish up into the second floor.

Heart racing, Olivia tossed the remote to the other side of the couch and said, "Come on, dude!"

The creaking of the stairs telegraphed a scramble up to the second floor.

As the hefty steps reached the hall above her head, she realized that even when he was running, the kid's light weight did not produce noises like these.

The slaps of feet, yes. But did the boy, a mere six years old, make such a racket the last time she caught him lurking on the stairs in preparation to shoot her with a dart gun or toss a homemade net on her?

Mouth set, Olivia glanced toward the ceiling of the eerie old house and willed her heart to settle down.

The house had settled down, too.

Though her palms were wet and she was overcome by the impulse to have Leroy over after all, Olivia knew she was being ridiculous.

This kind of thing happened all the time at the

Watson house.

She had never asked Luther because she didn't want to scare him; she hadn't asked the Watsons because they hadn't brought it up. They'd think she was some kind of nut.

But many nights, usually the nights when Mr. and Mrs. Watson were out especially late, the Watson house seemed to be awake.

At first she really thought it was the house settling. A floorboard would groan or a door would close hard after being caught in a draft.

Then, it became other things.

Sounds like footsteps, for example.

On a braver night, the third or fourth time such a thing happened, Olivia had turned the house upside-down. She had checked every corner, peeked in every room, stuck her head up in the family's dusty old attic.

Absolutely nothing was ever amiss. No sign of a break-in, or of anybody living in the house surreptitiously. There was never anything wrong on a night like this. By now, it was just an accepted hazard of the job that noises were occasionally going to happen while she was watching the Watson boy.

Besides...she had always understood that when you were dealing with...something beyond explanation... the best way to make it go away was to ignore it. Respond unemotionally. Treat it like a moth.

A very large, occasionally tangible moth.

So, Olivia had come into the custom of paying no

mind to the sounds that echoed now and again. Even when they frightened her, she put on a brave face and ignored them until they went away. And they always went away.

But she had never *seen* anything with those sounds before.

That was what made this instance so especially alarming.

Could it be that, all this time, the boy really had been behind the sounds? That was the most logical explanation. Usually the kid was fast asleep when the noises were at their most disturbing, but now she had some doubts.

With her phone's flashlight setting on, Olivia pushed the textbook from her lap and found herself wishing the Watsons had a dog she could send upstairs before her.

"Luther?"

The boy slept in his bedroom with a night-light and had briefly waged a war to keep the hall light on, but Olivia found he tended to stay in his room if the hallway was dark. For just a few seconds, the college student understood why. She hovered at the bottom of the stairs, her plaid shirt suddenly very thin protection as she cast the weak beam of the phone's flashlight into the upstairs corridor.

Nothing, of course.

One hand on the banister, Olivia crept up the staircase and listened for movement in the boy's room. She could usually hear him thump out of the bed and onto the floor or vice versa—that slap of feet again, plus a squeak in the mattress—but there was nothing now.

By the time she reached the second floor hallway, the house was so silent she had to ask herself what exactly she thought she was doing.

Luther's door was still closed. Olivia moved toward it on soft steps. She was sure he was still in there, but she had to satisfy her own doubt if she didn't want the Watsons to come home and find an empty bed to her later horror.

The flashlight aimed at her feet, Olivia reached for the knob.

Behind her, a bathroom slammed open.

Someone rushed along the hall and down the stairs, the heavy thunder of their footsteps chilling Olivia's blood.

"Luther! You scared me—Luther?"

But the thunder continued, rushing through the Watsons' living room and to the connected kitchen.

By the time Olivia had reached the top of the stairs, the fleeing boy had reached the back door. It slammed as it flew open, so loud to the aggrieved babysitter that even from another floor it seemed to mute her profanity.

"Luther! Where are you going?"

Taking the stairs two at a time, Olivia jetted through the house and cried out upon emerging in the kitchen.

As she feared, the back door hung open to a grim black view of the yard; and beyond that, the treeline marking the Watson property.

"Oh, fudge," said the babysitter to herself, stopping at the doorway and looking down at her phone. "Fudge, fudge—"

Her shaking hand cast the flashlight's beam out, but it could not reach the woods already echoing with broken twigs and howling wind. The urge to call the police was immediate and powerful, but then in rushed the frantic problems with that idea. Namely, losing her gig forever because she let the kid she was babysitting escape the house and get into the woods behind their neighborhood.

Groaning, Olivia ran a hand over her face, at least had the frame of mind to crack the door shut behind her, and rushed into the woods with the phone's flashlight flooding left and right.

Trees—lots, and lots of trees, all of them as black in the night as the backdrop of the stars.

"Luther?"

To avoid attracting the attention of neighbors for now, Olivia settled for projecting her whisper rather than shouting. No doubt, the boy could hear it all the same. He was probably lurking behind some tree, dressed as the grim reaper or some sci-fi villain, ready to spring out and laugh his little ass off when he finally got a real scream out of her. The kid had pulled some elaborate pranks before, but this one was just unacceptable.

"You think this is funny, you little twerp?"

Still whispering, Olivia scanned the area around while marching deeper into the trees. Grim shadows added to the obscurity of the ground, making her limited knowledge of tracking all the more useless.

The wind howled low, penetrating her flannel shirt and raising goosebumps along her arms.

"There's nothing funny about this," she summarized in answer to her own question. "You could get hurt, and we could both get in trouble. Come out! Luther? Come out right this very minute or I'm going to *have* to talk to your parents about what you did!"

She received no response except from the wind, which slowly raised in intensity.

Gritting her teeth, Olivia searched around for another sign of Luther and found none in her immediate proximity.

Her frustration peaked.

"So you want to stay out here in the cold?" Reverse psychology was a risky tactic, but it was better than stumbling blindly in the woods. "See if I care—play your little game for as long as you want. But when you finally realize you've messed up and you're all alone in the dark, scary woods by yourself, go ahead and scream. I'll come find you."

The wind's ominous howl picked up its intensity, its volume and pitch both increasing.

Chilled, Olivia turned in the direction she believed to be that of the house.

Through the darkness and its many trees, she

searched for signs of the kitchen lights still glowing through the Watsons' rear windows.

Olivia was just imagining herself in that kitchen, calling Leroy up to ask for his help in finding the kid, when she at last located the windows in the distance: two pinpoints of gold light.

Only when she took a step forward did she realize the lights were not windows.

They were eyes.

1

SOMETHING HARD STUNG the back of Luther's neck. He slapped his hand over the spitball's nasty little welt while shooting a look over his shoulder at Fliebolt.

The snickering bully gave him the finger, then put on the angel routine when a field trip chaperone turned around to inspect the fidgeting line.

Paine emitted a low growl. "Are you really sure you don't want to let me kill them?"

"There's a difference between want and should," Luther told his friend. "And, anyway—I get it."

"Get what?"

"I mean, I understand why they're jerks. We're different. It freaks them out."

"It shouldn't."

Luther shrugged, his gaze skipping away from his tall companion and across the sidewalk.

While he appreciated Paine's protective nature, things were starting to get a little...concerning. These kinds of reactions were just Paine's instinct, and Luther understood that, but he was starting to wonder if he wasn't going to have to sit his best friend down and have a real conversation. Murder was just not socially acceptable. Did Paine want them both to be seen as *real* weirdos?

Bigger real weirdos, anyway...weird enough to go to prison.

So far as Luther was concerned, it was dumb luck they weren't already seen that way.

A teacher from the class next door was given pause on her way to the back of the line. With a faltering smile, she bent before Luther.

"Are you really sure it's a good idea to take your doggie with you on the field trip, honey?"

Ugh. This was why he hated mixed field trips. You got all the other teachers and parents trying to baby you because they didn't know any better...he was in fourth grade, people.

"He's a wolf," said Luther of Paine, who did not reply on his own behalf since he was pretending to be a stuffed animal. While Luther shifted the beast from one arm to the other, lightly squeezing the slightly stringy fur that convincingly passed as store-bought faux stuff, Luther added, "And he can take care of himself."

"Oh, but what if he gets lost?"

"He won't."

"But—"

"Why don't you talk to my teacher?" Luther pointed at Mrs. Johnson and then stared forward in line, hoping that would put an end to the conversation. Still, the nervous teacher went on hassling.

"I'm sure he makes you feel much more comfortable, but you'll be safe with us! The museum is two hours away—if something were to happen—"

"Luther's not going to lose Paine, Ms. Viola."

Stacy Tifton had appeared in Luther's periphery, her smile small and forced as the one he gave her in return.

"He brings him everywhere these days," said Stacy in a way that was truth as much as insult. "He's used to it. Why, I think Paine's come on every field trip we've had since second grade!"

"What am I supposed to do? Leave him at home?"

Ms. Viola licked her lips, looking on the verge of saying that such a thing sounded like a good idea. But, when a teacher at the head of the line blew a whistle to wrangle the children, the adults straightened up the fastest—Ms. Viola included. Luther blew a sigh of relief while, her programming triggered by the whistle, the teacher hurried to the front of the line with her clipboard in-hand.

"All right, everyone!" Mrs. Johnson clapped her hands while she announced to the two classes and their volunteer chaperones, "Your folder should have a bus number on it. I want you all to make sure you're in the line for the right bus, and I want you to get on one at a time. Ms. Viola will check your name off the attendance list."

"Thanks, Stacy," said Luther grudgingly under his breath. "I thought she was really going to make me put him in the coat room."

"I couldn't let that happen! Then you'd look normal, instead of like a weirdo who talks to his stuffed animal."

While the mean girl chortled stupidly, Luther rolled his eyes with the full-sized wolf who had resumed looming over him again. The line jerked forward and Luther told her, "Well, all the same, thanks."

Paine nudged the human boy. "You think I should let her see me, Luther? Wouldn't she scream!"

"Don't do that."

"You're already talking to it!" Laughing softly to herself, Stacy shook her dirty blonde pigtails and told him, "It's funny and all, but I sort of feel bad for you. You're so attached to that thing that you can't see how embarrassing it is."

"I'm a kid, okay? Jeez. You could stand to act a little more like a kid sometimes, Stacy."

"I 'act' like myself—and, anyway, who could want to act like a kid? Don't you want to be a grown-up, Luther? Are you going to carry that toy around with you when you're working in an office?"

Luther didn't want to work in an office. Neither did Paine. While the wolf feigned gagging at the mere thought of being dragged to a place like that every day, Luther shrugged his shoulders and told the girl, "Maybe I won't work in an office. What do you care what I'm going to do? Why does it bother you?"

An irritated look crossed Stacy's face. Of all weird things, she seemed to blush—maybe that was just the sunburn from standing outside, though. As her freckled nose wrinkled in a bizarre kind of disgust that Luther couldn't parse, the girl said, "Well—of course, I don't *care*. I just mean—I just mean to say— oh, forget it."

Stacy's hazel eyes were drawn toward the calls of her friends a few people up. Shaking her head, the girl said, "You're hopeless, Luther," and hurried back to the girls who were already almost on the bus.

Sighing in relief to be alone with his true friend, Luther arched a brow at the wolf.

"What was *that* about?"

"I think she likes you," Paine said, pinching the human's cheek. While the boy laughed in surprise, Paine continued, "She does! I can tell. Why don't you ask her out? I'd swear to be good if it meant you could take her to a movie."

"Take her to a movie? I'm nine!"

"So? By the time I was nine, I was already married for the second time."

"Yeah, but you're a wolf!"

"I fail to see the difference it makes."

"So, you grew up faster. Like I told Stacy, I'm a kid. I'm too young for stuff like love. I just want to hang out with you."

"Ah, you can be love and still hang out with me. The right girl will love us both, anyway."

Maybe. Ideally. It was a nice pipe dream, as Luther's engineer father would have said, but the boy wasn't deluded. He knew the world saw him carrying on extensive, ostensibly one-sided conversations with his stuffed wolf.

That was ultimately why Luther didn't want Paine to kill anybody on his account. Legal implications aside, it didn't seem fair. Was Brock really to be held responsible for his inability to perceive a being that was, if not paranormal, certainly in some way ultranormal?

That was not to say Luther would have felt sorry if something terrible happened to his bully, or any of the feckless toadies constantly licking his heels. Right before it was his turn to check in with Ms. Viola, another stinging spitball glanced the ridge of his ear. Hissing, Luther resolved to ignore it—

But Paine's black lips pulled back from his fangs, his eyes shining red with bloodlust.

"That's it—"

Luther gasped. "No!"

Forgetting all composure in his panic, his mind flying with infinite and infinitely terrible envisionings of what could happen if Paine was set loose, Luther held the snarling wolf back from the children it wanted to devour.

"Remember what I told you. Please, Paine, don't hurt anybody today!"

As Paine continued snarling, incoherent with rage on his human friend's behalf, the area around grew quiet.

Mrs. Johnson cleared her throat. Paine, who tended to be a bit of a suck-up for adults he decided to like, stopped growling and perked his ears.

"Everything all right, Luther?"

Although Mrs. Johnson's tone was even, being used to, if not Paine, then Paine's keeper, Ms. Viola looked wide-eyed with shock. Maybe a little nervous. Could she see Paine? Probably not...just a weird kid, being weird.

"Sorry, Mrs. Johnson," said Luther as his teacher waved him onto the bus and told his name to her colleague, "I just got lost in thought."

Still rubbing his ear, Luther greeted the bus driver with a nod and maintained his frown until a bright spot cut through the fog in his morning.

The back seat was open!

That was a good sign. Maybe this trip wouldn't be so miserable after all. Feeling excited for the opportunity to sit with Paine and Paine alone, Luther hurried down the aisle with his sights set on—

"Hey, Luther! Sit with us!"

The boy's stomach sank. The downright demonic girls had divided across two seats: Stacy patted the seat in front of her and Luther cast one last reluctant glance at the back.

"Hurry up, Watson," somebody said behind him, giving him a shove when he delayed.

Luther shot Dingus (so the toady was called by Brock) a look that could kill as he slid into the the open space. While the crudely laughing group of bullies jostled each other on their way past him to the spot that could have been so peaceful for the two hour-long ride, Stacy leaned over the back of this lesser seat. Jessica, another girl of her circle, sat beside him to keep him blocked in with them. Terra grinned in a shitty way from around the side of the seat.

In futile self-defense, Paine sat between Luther and his seat-mate.

"So," said Stacy, her eyes bright with malice, "tell them about your friend."

2

MIRANDA STARED BLANKLY out the window until the bus came to a stop at the Smokeland Science Museum, where a number of buses and cars from other schools already filled the lot.

Had they really needed to drive? The museum was only a little over a mile from the school. Maybe two. What was the point of taking a bus, or for that matter a car, when her school was in the exact same small town and therefore practically adjacent to the museum?

"All right everyone," said Mrs. Carraway with more genuine interest than she had yet expressed for any outing that fall, "let's get ready for an adventure! Does everyone have their science questions to answer by the end of the day?"

"Yes," answered the class in disjointed unison.

Miranda sniffed lightly and slid her pencil into the seat before her.

She already knew the answers to the questions, just like she knew why the kids had been shuttled via bus to their destination. It was because half the parent chaperones—and quite a few of the teachers—were mostly too fat to walk. All of them seemed to have some variation of ailment. Diabetes; thyroid problems; pregnancy. Most of them set poor physical examples for the students.

Then, there was Mrs. Carraway, who was in very good shape, but who had obviously gone into teaching because it was the only thing she could think of at the time somebody asked her what she wanted to be when she grew up. In other words...Mrs. Carraway was somebody who had obtained her degree and gotten herself a job, only to realize that she didn't particularly like children.

At least in that way Miranda found her relatable.

Miranda let the rest of the class file out before she turned in her worksheet, mostly because she knew Mrs. Carraway would be hard to deal with. When the teacher looked down the bus one last time to see if everyone had gotten off, Miranda rose from her seat and smoothed her dress.

The teacher's bright expression tightened at once, her genuine smile transforming into a frigid, false little mask.

"Don't fall behind, now, Miranda! Let's not miss the start of our tour..."

"I have the answers for you."

The teacher blinked in annoyance and confusion, saying through her professional smile, "Excuse me?"

"The answers."

Miranda closed the distance and presented her teacher with the worksheet, telling her, "I have the answers to your worksheet, Mrs. Carraway. It was easy."

"Was it, now!"

Her tone as strained as her facial expression, the teacher glanced apologetically at the waiting bus driver and said, "But there are some things you have to experiment with to—"

"Yes, and I remember what they were like from the last two times the school sent us here…not to mention from basic knowledge. Do you really think the others don't already know what viscosity is?"

"Uh—well, Miranda, you certainly are…something!" Her unsmiling eyes crossing over the front and back of the sheet, barely reading the answers to confirm they were correct (they were), the teacher assured her student, "I'm glad you feel comfortable with the material, but don't you think it would be more fun to—you know, play along with the activities?"

"I would prefer I not make anyone uncomfortable," Miranda said simply. "For instance, I think I had better get off of the bus now, because I can tell you are increasingly disturbed by this conversation."

Her made-up eyelids rapidly batting, Mrs. Carraway stuttered. "Oh, well—well of course not, Miranda. It's just—"

"I will see you during the tour, Mrs. Carraway."

The teacher made a strangled little noise in the back of her throat, like she wanted to protest but couldn't come up with motivation enough to formulate a lie.

Miranda understood. Aside from her family being a notoriously eccentric bunch of Smokeland well-to-dos, Miranda did not talk down to teachers—or, for that matter, to students. Rudimentary games that she played all the time with her brother seemed to upset them, like the time she shaved Erica Still's hair off while playing Death Row, or the time she enlisted a few of her coevals to serve as components of her performance art recreation of Golgotha.

Unfortunately for that latter, very worthy artistic experiment, the Girl Scouts of America did not look kindly upon her vision and asked her not to return. Her parents were furious that the organization could not see their daughter's creative genius—and a little proud.

"Great artists are never accepted in their time," her father told her, clapping her on the shoulder amid a hearty handshake before handing what was not her first cigar.

"Perhaps you should come up with a new piece—'The Girl Scout Massacre.'" Her mother had stopped playing her harpsichord just to deliver the advice, delicate hands pausing upon the keys.

Yes, it was a good suggestion Miranda's mother had with that...but, truth be told, Miranda had long ago become aware of how different and strange a place the world was. All the normal aspects of human existence—interest in straitjackets, taxidermy, deadly insects, voodoo dolls—was considered 'niche' or 'strange' by the world at large. Even interesting subjects like birth defects or natural disasters seemed to upset people.

To Miranda, however, all these things were simply fascinating expressions of something unspeakable. That unspeakable thing was the one thing she had not begun to grasp at her young age. Math and science, writing and reading, all the history of the world: she absorbed everything, but still could not answer that bottommost question.

Why? Why was life distinct from death? Was it distinct from death only so as to *experience* death—or did it exist for more?

Miranda puzzled over existential questions constantly and could not hold her drifting attention to the lame lectures of her latest teacher. Sort of embarrassing...only three months into the school year, and Miranda was once again having fantasies of graduating early. Maybe, if she tried hard enough, she could still convince her parents to let her take that college entrance exam.

"I'm begging you, Roger, don't do this to me!"

The cry stirred Miranda from her somnambulist state. She came to in the middle of the pathway to the front doors of the museum, where her peers had congregated. A few attempted to climb the geology-themed rock wall nearby. As someone lost their grip on the jaw of a poorly recreated Tyrannosaurus Rex skull, the chaperone cried out and rushed to fuss over them. All the other adult heads turned in their direction.

Ignoring this, drawn toward the world of adult drama, Miranda ducked off the path and into the hedges beside the side door. There, a conversation was taking place. An old man who was obviously a janitor talked to a guy with black hair and thickly framed glasses—the boss, it would seem. He hushed the nearly tearful employee.

Or ex-employee.

"You can't do this to me, Roger."

"I'm sorry, Claude—you know I am. I just have to let you go. Nothing's getting cleaned around here if the rest of us aren't doing it, and—"

"I can change!"

"We've given you plenty of time to change. And it's not just the cleaning, like I was trying to say before you interrupted me."

While the janitor fell quiet, Roger lowered his voice to such an extent that even a pro eavesdropper like Miranda strained to hear.

"It's the supplies, Claude. You're stealing the supplies, and you have been for months! Bleach? Toilet paper? And I don't even want to know if you're the one who made that jar of hydrochloric acid disappear the other month."

Hydrochloric acid! What was that doing in a children's science museum?

At last, Miranda's imagination had been captured. Here she'd been thinking the day would be pointless. Now there was something fun to do! An experiment to run. How quickly and how well could hydrochloric acid burn a hole in the floor of the museum, for instance? What about this rock wall model in the front yard of the establishment— would it burn all the way through? Probably not, but it would still be fun to see what it did to Mr. Rex.

If only she had some organic material to test!

While Miranda pondered over the possibilities, the janitor stuttered out predictable denials. This Roger guy, having little to none of it, shook his head and affected another deep sigh.

"I'm sorry, Claude, I really am. We just can't have you around here anymore."

"At least let me get my belongings from my office."

Roger shook his head.

"We changed the office locks last night...the board decided it best if you don't spend time here unsupervised, and you don't want me hovering over your shoulder while you pack up a box of your stuff, do you? Just let me pack everything up for you...you know I'll get everything."

"Sure, but—"

"Don't worry about it, okay? I talked them into a little severance for you, since you've worked here so long."

"It's not about the damn money!"

The janitor's voice leapt up again. Miranda's heart raced with the thrill of conflict. Would there be a fight? This was great.

"I don't care about the money," said the janitor sharply. "I don't like this insult, and I don't like somebody else touching my things."

"You know I wouldn't intrude on your privacy, Claude."

"Damn it, Roger, I want my stuff and I want it now."

Roger cleared his throat and stole a quick look in the direction of the students. Miranda retreated into the shadows of the hedge whose branches embraced her just well enough to keep the stranger from seeing her. After a hefty sigh for the waiting tour group, Roger's expression grew stern.

He shook his head.

"I'm sorry, Claude, it's out of my hands. There's nothing I can do."

"'Nothing you can do!' Nothing the director of the museum can do...fuck that." Spitting at Roger's feet, the old man gave him the finger. "Nothing you *want* to do, you mean. Keep your severance package and choke on it. I don't want none of your goddamn money."

While Roger looked down at his feet, clearly in a state of shock for the classless response to adversity, the janitor swept in close and bared his mean little dentures.

"I know a thing or two about you, Roger Garnet. Don't think I couldn't ruin your career with a hard word or two."

Though he looked just taken aback enough to make Miranda think there was something to this claim, the director narrowed his eyes behind his spectacles.

"I think you should go now."

Muttering some unpleasant words, the maligned janitor stalked off to his car. The director watched, his mouth hard and his arms folded.

Miranda glowed with the vigor of an energy vampire, flush with the intoxication of a secondhand conflict.

What fun! That guy sure was angry to have the director sorting out his things. Did he have something he shouldn't in that office? Janitors usually did—at least, in fiction they did. Miranda tapped her chin. Probably just adult magazines, or something...but maybe there was something more interesting than anything like that.

Well, there was only one way to discover what this old man didn't want anyone to know about.

Break into his office and snoop around.

Sounded like the first step would be getting the key from Roger, or Roger's office...but maybe that was the second step.

It was hard to pull off a heist by oneself, after all. What Miranda needed was a conspirator.

Or a patsy.

Dusting herself off, Miranda stepped out of the bushes and didn't even earn a second look from her distant classmates. Much as she was used to them, they were used to her and didn't think to laugh to see her coming out of a hedge. Normally she would have been more discreet anyway, but her mind was preoccupied as she considered her options.

Unfortunately, most of her peers were wise to her ways. They knew that, if they were going to be invited to help her with something, it would be something dangerous, illegal, or both. They definitely wouldn't be willing to play lookout for her while she rifled through the janitor's things, and they *absolutely* wouldn't take a fall unless they were an individual too meek or bad-natured to avoid becoming a suspect in the crime.

But, let's face it…everybody at Runner Elementary knew that if Miranda Even was involved in an incident, she had probably orchestrated the whole thing, too. That included peers, as well as teachers.

And that was why, as the buses of some other school system pulled into the parking lot of the museum, Miranda smiled.

3

THE TRIP WENT as expected, and Luther hated every second of it. He would have much rather sat there banging his head against the window for two hours than be forced to answer questions about Paine—or on Paine's behalf—while these annoying girls giggled and exchanged glances and egged him on as though he were doing some kind of improv routine for their entertainment.

"I notice you aren't gagging to kill *them,*" Luther wryly muttered to his friend while the girls whispered to each other.

"Of course not! Don't you love the attention? Ladies love a little Paine."

While the wolf buffed his black claws against the fur of his chest, his lips curling back from his teeth in a fangy smile, Luther rolled his eyes. "I doubt that."

"Nah, trust me…you'll find out when you're older."

The girls broke their conversation as though prompted by the boys' exchange of whispers.

"So what does he eat, then?"

"I told you already."

"But your mom doesn't mind all that raw hamburger going to waste?"

"It's not going to waste. I just told you, he's eating it."

"Yeah, but—"

The bus stopped short at a clogged intersection and the girls were jostled in their seats, with Jessica in particular smashing into the seat before them. While Luther and Paine howled in laughter and Stacy told him sourly, "That's not funny," the teachers at the front of the bus began to whistle for attention.

"All right, everybody! We're almost there and we're a little behind, so I want you to get out of the bus and go straight to the tour. It should be at the front of the building—Ms. Viola will go out first and stand with her pink clipboard in the air so you can find her. Wherever she is, meet her. Clap if you understand."

While the whole bus clapped with varying degrees of enthusiasm, Mrs. Johnson nodded and slid back down into her seat. "This should be fun! Remember to meet back up with me after the tour so we can decide who's going to start where—we don't want to have everybody crowding into one section at once!"

The bus muttered semi-agreeably as it cruised

on through the blockage. Luther looked somewhat pleadingly at Paine while the girls, soured on the game of making fun of the class weirdo, now whispered to each other around seat's edge.

Luther sighed. "Please tell me today is going to be a better day than I think it is."

Paine lifted his muzzle as though scenting the wind. "Mm, I don't know...I've got a pretty good feeling about it."

That made one of them.

One thing that was nice was Smokeland itself. Luther didn't like the drive, but he enjoyed field trips there because the town's food was good and the activities were fun. He hadn't been to the science museum before and hoped it wouldn't be too patronizing, but also not too dry. There was a balance to be struck...he wanted to try to make the most of even a bad situation, and since every day with his rude classmates was a pretty bad situation, he was especially devoted to finding bright spots.

Luther and Paine sprang off the bus one at a time, the wolf flashing a smile at the driver before stooping beneath the door with a yawn and a stretch. As his long arms raised above him, his ears pinned back with the force of his yawn.

"Phew, that was some drive! I don't know about you, Luther, but I'm ready to run around."

"Yeah, well, sounds like we're gonna have to wait awhile..."

Not to mention fight for space. Luther was a little annoyed at the size of the tour group already developing from some other class of some other school; one of several who would inevitably hog all the cool offerings of the museum.

But one of their number fixed him with her stare.

The darkest bright spot he'd ever seen.

Luther stopped in place while meeting eyes with the dark-haired girl whose neat bob was sci-fi short and ornamented with a big red bow that tucked her hair back from her proud forehead. The fringes of her lashes made her brown eyes look huge even at a distance, and the pale hue of her skin was so extraordinary that his first thought was she looked like the moon.

Luther's heart skipped a beat and his eyes immediately averted. While the boy receded into himself, the wolf slapped him in the arm while asking, "What's wrong?"

"That girl," whispered Luther. "She's looking at me."

"Who—oh! That girl? Say...no she isn't."

One great paw shading his surprised eyes, Paine wagged his tail and said with delight, "I think she's looking at *me!*"

Luther's head whipped up again.

Paine was right. The girl's placid stare had been replaced by a look of profound astonishment. Her widening eyes were now trained up at Paine's height, but the idea that she could actually see the wolf still seemed impossible. After years of family, teachers, and peers all treating him like he was developmentally delayed because of their inability to see his friend, it had been determined that nobody could see Paine but Luther.

"That can't be," decided the boy with a shake of his head, marching on without waiting for his friend. "It hasn't happened yet, and it's never going to happen."

"I wouldn't be so sure..." The wolf barked. Quickly, he laughed. "See! She jumped."

With another, sharper glance, Luther assessed the girl. Her fascinated gaze trailed back to Luther. The boy found himself stopping in place again.

While he tried to figure out what he was going to do, some teacher from the other school called for attention.

As her peers all obediently turned their heads, the girl looked on.

Her lips pursed.

Only with great reluctance did she turn away from him, her hands folded at the back of her black, peter pan-collared dress with the occasional impatient twitch.

"She definitely saw me," said Paine. "One hundred percent."

"But why her?" Frustration swept over Luther at the possibility. "Why not somebody from my family— Mom and Dad, or even one of my cousins?"

Paine shrugged his great shoulders. "Beats me...only one way to find out, though! You gotta talk to her."

Luther made a pathetic, strangled noise, falling into the crowd of the peers who had gathered around and were now being shepherded to the rest of the tour by Ms. Viola.

"I *can't* talk to her," said Luther.

Paine grinned. "Because you think she's cute?"

"What? No! Because people think I sound crazy when I talk about you. That's why Stacy wanted me interpret all those answers from you on the ride here. They were making fun of me."

"Mm, I don't know...sounds to me like you've got a crush!"

"What part of *anything* I just said makes you think I have a crush on anyone?"

"It's not your words," said Paine, prodding Luther in the chest with a claw sharp enough to make the boy grimace. "It's your heart! That pulse of yours is *flying*. Makes me want to chase you down and maul you like a spring lamb!"

The wolf grinned while the boy cleared his throat in a futile effort to hide both his fear of his friend's strength and his crush on this strange girl (not-crush, that was, of course).

"I'm trying to listen to the teacher," muttered Luther, which was of course total BS.

The truth, however, was that there was nothing much to listen to. This guy with black hair and glasses who had been talking to the other groups' teachers now stood up in front of everyone and welcomed them to the Smokeland Science Museum, where everybody was invited to be a scientist for a day, blah blah…

Yeah, it was probably a cool speech that captured the imagination, and this 'Bill' guy who delivered it did so with enthusiasm and eyes bright with excitement for the day ahead, but Luther couldn't focus on a single word any adult was saying.

His brain felt a way it never had before; like a thousand ants were crawling along the insides of his skull. Between that and his thudding heart, he actually felt a little dizzy. Was he going to pass out? Did he need to sit down?

No. He had to act like everything was fine. After all, what if he passed out and this girl saw? What would she think of him?

Not that he cared.

But what if she was cool, and they could have been friends, but because he passed out in front of her like a total dweeb she didn't want to hang out with him?

Worse…what if she just didn't like him? Then he would have to rewrite his entire personality, because that would be the final proof there was something wrong with it.

Wait, no, ugh!

Why was he thinking like this?

Luther lifted a hand to his forehead, no more able to banish thoughts of the mysterious girl than he was able to keep himself from somehow feeling her presence—as though a great, black planet with its own gravitational field now loomed somewhere behind his right periphery.

And, second by second, that gravity grew more intense.

What was it about her? Was she *really* so special? Maybe she wasn't even looking at Paine. She must have been reading the name of Luther's town on the bus, or watching somebody else coming down the stairs behind him.

She probably wasn't even that cute. Not really.

Luther decided he'd better check, just to make sure.

Subtly, though.

Hands sliding into the pockets of his blue windbreaker, Luther put on a show of looking around as though he were bored, or perhaps simply curious. His gaze wandered off to the left, then up and around… down at his feet, then over his right shoulder—

Where the girl had filtered into his classmates as though able to blend seamlessly, though she was anything but nondescript. She was unapologetically focused on him. Now that they had locked eyes, he felt compelled to look back.

Even if looking back made him so nervous that he thought he was going to puke.

"Just stay calm, buddy," coached the big wolf, nudging Luther's shoulder.

Her eyes flashed toward the wolf's muzzle, then the motion of his paw.

Luther wheezed in anxiety. Free of her gaze, he whipped his head back to the museum director's cheerful suggestion that they follow him inside and get to know some of the exhibits.

The science museum was probably cool, but this girl's deal, whatever it was, could not be quantified via scientific models. It was clear to Luther that she was something else—what precisely, he couldn't be sure. A witch, maybe—or a vampire.

Luther's private questions continued to swirl as the classes were given a broad overview of the museum. The director gestured around him while, above his head, a pingpong ball pressurized by a few students shot through a track along the ceiling and gave Luther something else to look at.

That was a cool replica rover hanging up there. Martian, or Lunar?

Golly, a Hall of Optical Illusions? You could spend hours there!

A giant spirograph machine? Fascinating. Simply—

"Hey."

The sharp, feminine whisper made Luther jump out of his skin.

As the director, Roger Something, went on pointing out the gift shop before leading everyone toward the main exhibit hall, Luther's head whipped toward the girl. She now stood almost directly behind him, like a jump scare in a video game.

Her alien features tightened in a serious way. She

jerked her chin toward the director, whispering, "Face forward or they'll notice."

Throat tight with multiple kinds of anxiety, Luther obeyed.

The girl sidled up beside him now, her slow migration complete.

"I'm Miranda," she whispered. "What's your name?"

"Luther," he whispered back.

"What's your friend's name?"

Miranda's eyes were trained up over his head now, but it didn't matter. Hot on the heals of his shitty bus ride and still suffused with disbelief that anyone could really see Paine, Luther held back a twinge of annoyance at the question.

"Why don't you ask him?"

"Okay. What's your name?"

The girl peered up at the wolf, and the wolf smiled back.

"Paine," he answered obligingly, "with an 'e.'"

"Like Thomas Paine," the girl remarked aloud in as soft a tone as she could use while still exhibiting interest. As Luther's jaw dropped, her gaze turned forward again. "Author of *Common Sense* and godfather of the United States. That's a strange person to name a wolf after, Luther."

"H—he named himself. You mean to say you can really see him?"

A chaperone shushed them in response to Luther's volume rising a little too high. Blanching, the boy waited while they all moved to the center of the main exhibit hall and the many stations he was too distracted to hear named. When attention had drifted away from the students, Miranda resumed whispering.

"That's right, I can see him. Can't you?"

"Well, sure! But nobody else can."

"Oh," she said in the bland way of someone who had been told something she already knew, "that's not surprising. I'll bet I know why, too."

"Why's that?"

"Because most people have no imagination," she answered sagely.

"The girl's right," agreed Paine with a nod. "A being like me can't be friends with just anybody, Luther. I tell you that all the time."

"Just *what* are you, sir?"

The girl's question made Paine laugh in a low tone that usually scared away the monsters under the bed. "You sure are pointed, kid…what am I? I'm Luther's friend, Miranda. I could be yours, too, if you wanted."

Miranda cast a distant look toward the teachers who pretended to listen slightly less successfully than the students. "I wouldn't want to step on any toes. But I could be friends with both of you, if you'd like."

"Yes," said Luther a little too quickly, his voice leaping in such an odd and embarrassing way that he took to coughing. A few people glanced over as he covered his mouth, but thought nothing of it. As they all looked away to follow the director to the final exhibit areas, Luther caught his breath.

"Yeah," he said more casually, "yeah, sure, that'd be cool. Or whatever."

Introduction ended, the groups went their separate ways. Miranda tarried to nod. "Cool. Meet me in the shadow room."

As she disappeared off to play the part of a student for a few minutes, Luther said without thinking, "Okay," then bolted to a straighter posture.

Crud! He basically ignored the entire tour. Where was that exhibit, again?

"Did you happen to catch where that was?"

Paine arched a cartoonish brow and, barking out a laugh, shook his great muzzle. "Brother, you got it *bad!* That's okay, you got me for a wingman. Pawman. Whatever. Too bad I wasn't paying attention, either."

Luther rolled his eyes while the wolf laughed. "Don't worry! The operation isn't doomed yet."

"'Operation!'"

"Our first step is figuring out what wing of the science museum she was talking about. Let's see..."

While, tapping his chin, the wolf wandered to read the signage displayed here and there, Luther stowed his annoyance at his friend and tried to remind himself the wolf wasn't teasing him. Not maliciously, anyway.

That was a good thing, because Luther had enough malicious teasing coming from his classmates.

"All right, everybody." With an oblivious smile, Ms. Viola clapped until all the students started clapping in rhythm with her. When attention was considered sufficient, she said, "Now's the fun part—I want you to go ahead and divide into groups of four, and explore the museum!"

"Don't forget to see me," reminded Mrs. Johnson with a hasty look her way.

The students cheered and locked eyes with their friends, usually the three closest people already closest to them.

In this case, Luther had no friends. Even Paine had wandered off, leaving the boy defenseless when Stacy and the other two slithered up with mean little smiles.

"You should join our group, Luther! It'll be fun."

"No," said the boy weakly, "that's okay, I'll just—"

"No!"

Stacy's eyes widened, fury burning in them to be rejected by the lamest boy in the class.

"Do you have another group to be in?"

"Well," he stuttered, "no, but—"

"Then, come on!"

Rolling her eyes in annoyance, Stacy grabbed him by the wrist.

All right, he wasn't crazy. She really was blushing.

Was Paine right about Stacy having a crush on Luther? But she was so mean! Girls made no sense to him at all.

Maybe Miranda would make sense, though.

Something about her seemed to indicate she would—maybe because he made sense to her, or *could* make sense to her. One way or another, her ability to see Paine held a definite promise.

If he could just figure out how to get away from his group and get to her!

4

MIRANDA WAITED IN the aptly-named shadow room for about ten minutes. In this time, her calculating mind struggled to come up with a suitable explanation for the perfection of what had just happened.

To say she could not believe her eyes would have been an exaggeration. Miranda knew she was not insane and did not have any kind of chemical or hormonal imbalance that could promote hallucinations. The things she saw had to be real.

It was still quite shocking, of course, to have been sizing up this somewhat anxious-looking, dark-haired boy, only to realize that the nearby person one had taken for a teacher in a dark coat and pair of trousers was actually a seven-foot-tall, gangly wolf walking on its hind legs and capable of perfect English. Shocking... but not completely unbelievable, since she saw it.

Since nobody from her school saw it, it was easy enough to draw the conclusion that the creature, though real, was possibly of inter-dimensional origin and/or a terrestrial being with the ability to bend light and possibly matter, thus appearing invisible or even intangible to the world around. Testing this hypothesis would be its own mission entirely, and perhaps an issue for another day.

Whatever the case, Miranda decided that she had ought to make her first-ever friend. Maybe if Luther stayed cute she would even marry him someday. Wouldn't that be nice?

Hm. Her father was always going on and on about how he knew as soon as he saw her mother that she would be his wife. Miranda always thought it was a bunch of bologna, but maybe she was wrong.

There was still a lot to settle in between now and then, though. Did he have a sense of humor? Would he do what she asked when it came to breaking into the janitor's office? Would he be weirded out if they found something truly inappropriate, or would he have a sense of humor about it?

All these things were important aspects of friendship suitability...however, regardless of the boy's personal virtues and flaws, he would always have one strong point in his favor.

It was hard to deny that the demonic or possibly alien friend really sold him...although there had to be something about the boy's personality to commend him.

When ten minutes turned into twelve, Miranda grew impatient. A group posing in the dark shadow room—where, every so often, a flash of light would freeze guests' shadows on the wall of light sensitive paint—leapt with terror as a body suddenly distinguished itself from a corner. Evidently they had taken Miranda, lost in thought, for some kind of mannequin. As they cried out, she emerged in the light of the main museum floor with a hand before her squinting eyes.

Ugh.

Children everywhere.

Miranda had just never gotten along with other children. Even her brother had his choice moments. Truth be told, he was more of a science project than a sibling, at least as far as Miranda's relationship to him went, but she guessed he was fun when it came to playing games and caring about her and so on. It was good to have a family that cared about her; they were all Miranda needed.

Especially when other children were on a different circuit of consciousness altogether.

While the kids around her allowed themselves to become engrossed in the museum, answering whatever questions their teachers had passed out, Miranda wandered in silence from exhibit to exhibit. All the while, she raked the crowds for the tall black wolf she soon found in the main exhibit hall. To see her coming his way, Paine perked and waved a great, black paw, then pointed to a bicycle where Luther pedaled away, visibly short of breath.

"Go, Luther, go, Luther!"

A group of three bland-looking girls stood around him, cheering and clapping as his exertions did everything from turn on a fan to activate a radio to send an electric model train chugging around the tracks above their head. While one of them said, "Make it go faster," and the others agreed, Luther's miserable gaze swept over the museum floor.

When he noticed Miranda, his relief was visible.

"Actually," he said, clambering down from the bike, "I think I have to go pee after that bus ride."

"TMI," said one of the brats, all three of them laughing in unison.

Miranda's eyelid twitched in annoyance. She ducked back around the corner and waited near the swinging doors of the restrooms a ways down the hall, her arms folded impatiently before her.

"People used to talk to me that way, too," explained Miranda gruffly when Luther came around the corner, still panting from the bike.

"How did—you make—them quit it—"

"Are you all right?"

"Just—a little—"

The gasping boy doubled over, leaving Miranda to sigh.

"Don't *bend*," she said, coming to draw him upright by means of a hand under his arm.

The boy cried out like he'd been shocked and Miranda withdrew.

"Are you all right?"

"Sorry! Uh, sorry, you just—surprised me."

Poor kid. When was the last time he'd been touched by surprise without it being a noogie, or a punch in the back of the head?

Or a wolf springing out at them.

Luther squawked when Paine leapt around and lunged upon the boy's back. The beast howled with laughter while Luther produced a scowl, saying harshly, "Not here!"

Seeing Miranda was unruffled, the laughing wolf began to calm.

"Aw, she doesn't scare easy!" Paine pouted, his ears flopped down along with his tail. "Shucks! That can be good in a friend, though."

"You shouldn't sneak up on people," Miranda advised, unimpressed. "You never know what's going to happen."

"I know what'll happen with Luther...he'll make me laugh!" The wolf giggled, ruffling the boy's hair, then looked toward a sudden inundation of perfume with a sniff. "Cheese it! The cops."

"Is everything all right over here, Miranda?"

Mrs. Carraway edged over, her hands wringing before her somewhat while she studied Miranda with the unfamiliar boy. Though Miranda assured her, "Yes," the teacher continued waiting for Luther to say something.

"Uh," he answered, glancing quickly at Miranda, "yeah, it's fine."

"Well...just let me know if you need anything. Are you from the other school?"

As Luther nodded weakly, Paine and Miranda shared a sidelong look of disapproval. Miranda knew only one way to get the teacher away: make her uncomfortable.

"Yes," said Miranda plainly. "This is my boyfriend, Luther."

"Boy—I'm sorry."

Like a computer rebooting, Mrs. Carraway's eyelids fluttered wildly. Clumps of mascara stuck together awkwardly. Why had this woman bathed in so much makeup and perfume today?

"Boyfriend," repeated the teacher, forcing another strange, strangled smile. "Boyfriend! Well...isn't that nice. Hm! Well...well, I'm actually going to take my lunch early so the others have time to enjoy *their* lunch later on, so if you need any help for the next thirty or forty minutes, just find a volunteer—okay?"

"I won't need help," Miranda said, although the teacher was plainly speaking to the still-sputtering "boyfriend."

While Mrs. Carraway wandered off, lightly shaking her head to herself as though over something mysterious, Miranda jerked her head toward a few classrooms available for dry ice and physics demonstrations. Not a moment too soon, either:

as they disappeared into the unlocked but empty auditorium, the roving gang of mean girls who had been harassing Luther came clucking around in pursuit of him.

"Where did he go to? Is he still peeing?"

"Maybe he ran away to be with his—"

Miranda tugged on the hydraulic door just a little bit to get it to close faster.

"Listen," said Luther, regaining his footing now that the three of them were alone, "I'm sure you're great, and everything, but I don't know you! Don't you think—"

"Are you saying you don't want to be my boyfriend?"

"I'm not saying *that*," said the boy, which pleased her; especially as he blushed to realize he had said it without thinking. Without acknowledging or correcting his own gaff, he continued, "I'm just saying—I'm saying that this is all happening a little fast! I don't even know what your *deal* is."

She shrugged. "There is no deal. Same as yours, I guess."

"No way." Shaking his head, Luther gestured to the door and dropped his voice with respect for the teammates passing by outside. "No way. There's something weird about you, too, if you can see Paine like I can—more than your imagination. If your teacher hadn't shown up just now, I would have started worrying you weren't real."

"Maybe my teacher's not real," posited Miranda, staring into Luther's soul.

"Now just you hold on—"

"Relax," Miranda replied, dropping the game because he was clearly too sensitive to gaslight for fun. "She's real, and you're real, and I'm real, and Paine is real."

"Sister, it sure is...oh, you mean me!" While the wolf laughed at his own joke, meandering to a white board at the head of the auditorium, the children ignored him.

"Okay, I thought so. I mean—you seem real." Luther nodded to himself before adding, "And it seemed like your teacher was nervous for some reason."

"Everyone at my school is nervous around me."

"Why?"

"Because one time I convinced a girl to set herself on fire, and everybody knows I did it but nobody could prove it."

Luther's eyes bugged from his head. "Are you messing with me again?"

"Am I?"

He searched her face, looking a little pale while the laughing wolf uncapped a marker and called, "That's a good one."

"You must be kidding," Luther decided, his tone still uncertain.

The corners of Miranda's lips twitched in a mysterious un-smile.

"I make people nervous in part because of my family. You really must not be around here—where are you from?"

"Griffon."

"I see." Nodding, Miranda said, "Then you haven't heard of the Evens."

"The Evans?"

"No, the Evens—as opposed to odds." As the boy nodded in understanding, Miranda explained, "It would probably be more accurate if we *were* the Odds. My mother grows only carnivorous or stinky plants, and my father actually had an ancient native American burial ground *installed* on the property a few years ago."

"Yikes," said the boy. "You can do that? But they were humans."

"I know," said the girl with a grim look. "My parents are not the most 21st century people, unfortunately. For Gen Xers, they act a lot like boomers."

"My parents, too."

Sighing, talk of parents no doubt making him think of responsibility, Luther looked at the auditorium's clock and said with a flop of the folder under his arm, "Look, um, Miranda, I'd really like to stay and talk, but I have to go answer these questions with my group. Maybe we could—"

"I left my pencil on the bus," Miranda said, taking the folder from his hand before he could pull it from reach. "Do you have one?"

"Huh? Well, uh, yeah—"

The boy dug his writing implement from his windbreaker pocket and extended it. When she took it, Luther's breath hitched at the contact of their fingers.

Miranda looked away.

"Have you ever had a crush on anyone before, Luther?"

"Uh—uh, that is—"

"Never mind," said Miranda, flipping open the folder and busying herself by skimming the contents of the first question. "Oh, these are easy. No math? Maybe one or two, looks like... Here, write this down."

Thrusting both pencil and folder back at him, Miranda waved him to the nearby auditorium desk while instructing him on the answer to the first question. The boy looked at her with amazement.

"How do you know that? Is that really the answer?"

"Yes, of course. I know it because I'm a scientist—now hurry up and write these answers. I've got something I need your help with."

"What's that?"

While the boy's pencil flew into motion, Miranda explained, "I think this place's former janitor has something to hide...and I'd like to find out what."

5

CLAUDE KRUMB'S KNUCKLES burned white as he drove home from the station, but his face was still blood red.

They'd barely even placated him, the bastards. They'd heard he had just been fired and they didn't even take a second to consider his complaint might be serious, even though it was obviously a goddamned serious complaint to be making. Even if it *had* been a lie, all possibility of it being valid was put aside in favor of assuming it was a revenge-based, malicious report.

And it had indeed been a revenge-based, malicious report...but it was one Claude had to make in order to cover his ass.

That nosy son of a bitch, Roger Garnet...he was right. The high motherfucker would love it if he knew, but it was a fact that the old man had been stealing things from work to help him at home. And why shouldn't he? Wasn't a man entitled to be supported by his employer in a time of dire need? Especially when he'd given his whole damn life—his soul!—to the company?

The janitor's limbs trembled with fury all the way home. That Sheriff Hayward bastard had been the worst. Hayward and one of his deputies had interviewed Claude themselves, and every question seemed aimed at discrediting rather than discovering.

"Are you really sure that's what you saw?"

"Don't you think you sound a little tired after the morning you've had, Claude?"

"What if we brought you back in tomorrow, once you've had a night to sort things out?"

They hadn't cared. They did claim to, claimed even that they would open an investigation based on what he'd said, but also claimed it would strengthen their case if he'd come back tomorrow. They couldn't make an immediate move without a lot of red tape being blown wide open.

In other words...they didn't believe him, because if they believed him they would have lain siege to the damn museum that very morning.

"What are you waiting for?" Claude had waved his hands, insisting, "If you've listened to a word I've said, you ought to be leaping in there, guns blazin'!"

"As much as we agree, Claude, you know that's just not how we do things...there's a process. Just come back tomorrow and we'll get some additional information out of you, okay?"

Hell, no.

Not okay.

Claude wouldn't be back to the police station tomorrow. He wouldn't be back there at all. Wouldn't be anywhere, ever.

Most everything was already at work, but he was fairly damn sure that his favorite was still at home.

Good thing, too. The whole point of this had been that he did *not* want to go out like a bitch. Hell! He'd even killed Janet because she'd found the notebook, and he *loved* Janet...when she did what he told her to.

Ironically, now that she was a corpse, he loved her more than he ever thought possible. She was quiet and docile and would do just about anything but properly, quickly decompose.

And that had been a problem for some time, but, well...he supposed it didn't matter anymore.

"They're gonna find me out," said the janitor, assessing his wife with a solemn tone, his hands in the pockets of his coveralls while he stood over a tub so rancid even the flies had not dared help themselves to its contents. The withered, black face of his dead wife stared back, her flesh having been mutilated not just by rot but by the hydrochloric acid whose use he abandoned after finding the damage it did to the tub beneath to be so extreme. Damn shame! It had done a good job on *her*, and ordering more from the museum's distributors would have been nothing at all.

He was still considering it at the time of his firing. He'd read up on that Dahmer fella and been planning on getting her a proper barrel of some kind, or trying to figure out some way to make a sort of glass casket out of a few old coffee tables...but this was so much easier.

"I know it seems like your death was a waste now," he continued to the body, "but, Hell, look at it this way...least you and I can be in Heaven together. No more waitin'."

The dead body continued baring its teeth up at its former husband, strings of congealed scalp still clinging to its skull. The putrefied woman's flesh had substantially softened from the moisture of the bathroom and the occasionally leaking tub. One had the sense it could slip free of bone at any moment, and would.

He had been so close to getting her out of this house and moving on with his life somehow...damn that bastard, Roger Garnet. Damn him!

There was just no other choice. Now that he was separated from the office, Claude was going to have the rug pulled out from all his plans. It would all be for nothing.

He had one way out.

Weakly sobbing the miserable tears of a man who was not truly mournful but only full of wretched, unreasonable self-pity, Claude covered his face with his hand and lurched out of the bathroom. After stabilizing himself somewhat in the hallway, heaving a great sigh and bravely fighting back further tears, the old man made his way to the bedroom he once shared with his beloved.

The bedside drawer stuck as he opened it, protesting his decision. He hesitated, wondering if this small resistance was some genuine sign from something divine.

But, of course, it wasn't. There was nothing Claude Krumb had ever found that made him believe in any kind of divinity. That was why he was the kind of person that he was.

That was why he slid the gun out from his nightstand. Because he was a humiliated, bitter man, crippled inside by his own decision to alienate himself; and, because he could not self-alienate as a religious hermit, he self-alienated as a violent psychopath.

"This is it," said the old man, bearing the gun to the violated bathroom. "All that's left."

From beneath the sink, Harvey removed the big glass decanter of acid pilfered from the museum. After studying it with some reluctance, than looking down at his wife, Claude redoubled his will. He set the container down to lay supine atop his moist soulmate, shivering at the way her desecrated remains squished and oozed beneath him.

"Excuse me, dear," he said softly. "This way, we can die together...maybe we won't even leave that much of a mess. I'll just turn on the tap here, that'll help us run down the drain...there"

Bending his knees with his feet flat on either side of hers, Claude set the glass container of acid on his knees and carefully removed the cap.

With the dangerous fluid just balanced, he reached for the gun still upon the seat of the shut toilet.

His plan had been to shoot himself in the head, thereby causing his legs to collapse, or the very least twitch. This would cause the acid to not only ensure the job was done right, but to perhaps reduce the process of clean-up for someone else. The thought of leaving a mess truly sickened Claude, who was deeply offended that the science museum thought to blame him, rather than the sticky children always putting their fingers all over the exhibits without being stopped by the adults around them.

But all thoughts of leaving anything flew away. Reaching for the gun caused the jar of acid to prematurely collapse, splashing across his face and hands and producing a sharp cry of agony. While the old man wailed, his face sizzled beneath an acid that tore open the lid of one eye and made short work of the now uncloseable eyeball. As Claude thrashed upon the eroding corpse of his wife, whose twisted hands also began to sear beneath the chemical burns, his vision failed and his skull burned with pain.

Was the acid getting into his brain? The agony was so great that his legs and arms thrashed out in all direction, his foot kicking hard enough to break against the faucet. Snapping bones were his last perception before time appeared to skip and his limp foot already lay bloody and broken in the tub. He'd had some sort of seizure, a realization he had only because he was now covered in vomit in addition to the blood still pouring from his face.

Gagging in pain, the old man groped around the toilet's lid. His fingers brushed the gun, but his haste to grab it knocked it down upon the floor.

Crying out, half-blind and still being actively mutilated amid some of the worst agony he had ever endure, Claude Krumb dragged himself out of the bathtub and fell into a soup of his own blood with a sob. He lay on the bathroom floor for a few long seconds before crawling the six inches required to reach the gun, a journey that might as well have been sixty miles.

At long last, his fingers brushed the gold metal.

Foaming at the mouth, blood dripping from his spittle covered lips, Claude lifted the gun to his temple, pointed the trigger, and fired.

It clicked.

Now he remembered why he hadn't brought this gun to work.

He'd meant to buy more ammunition.

6

LUTHER HAD TO admit…as much as he liked Miranda, he just wasn't sure about her idea of a good time.

"Are you positive we won't get into trouble for this?"

Miranda looked at him in a screwed-up way, her nose wrinkling in annoyance. Looking as though she tried to decide what to say to him, she looked back to the worksheet she double-checked without more comment than, "We can only get into trouble if we're caught. That's why we have to go *together*—to watch each other's backs."

Sighing as they reached the bottom of the basement stairs and the hall of subterranean offices below the science museum, Luther exchanged a look with Paine. The wolf grinned and gave him a thumb's up, for whatever that was worth with a dewclaw.

Maybe Luther had been better off sticking with his group and doing his assigned work at the pace he was supposed to...it was just, Miranda was so smart and pretty, and she knew just what to say to get people to do things.

"Tell them you came to the museum this summer so you already knew all the answers," she said, thrusting the folder back into his hands. "While you're at it, ask for permission to hang out with me. That way you won't get in trouble if that group of nitwits torturing you earlier try to give you a hard time."

So, while Miranda waited some feet away, that was what he did. Mrs. Johnson looked over his work with a skeptical air at first, but by the back page her eyebrows had lifted.

"I have to say I'm awfully impressed," she confessed. "Why didn't you raise your hand when I asked who had been here before?"

"I just forgot," lied the boy to a teacher who viewed him as largely honest, and therefore disregarded the possibility he might be lying.

Now that lie sat with him guiltily, but...there had been worse crimes in the history of the world. He would make up for it, hopefully.

For now, Luther was free to explore the grounds of the science museum with his new friend—within reason, of course.

And was breaking into some old janitor's office really within reason?

Some people were used to getting into trouble. Luther was certainly used to it, what with Paine always doing bizarre, sometimes dangerous things to and around him, and the antics he had once gotten up to of his own impetus…but there was trouble, and then there was Capital-T "Trouble."

Getting in trouble for daydreaming in class or shooting Stacy with rubber bands was a far cry from going on a field trip and getting busted for breaking into an office.

"I don't know about this," he muttered as they made their way down the long, white hallway of the basement, first in pursuit of the director's office and whatever spare keys he had apparently claimed from the janitor that morning, or something. Luther wasn't sure on the details and couldn't help but continue uncomfortably asking, "What if we get caught? They'll never let me go on a field trip again!"

Miranda rolled her eyes, the effect exaggerated by the impossibly large size of the sockets in her round skull. "That would be a tragedy. What would you do if you couldn't go to the zoo for the four thousandth time?"

"I love the zoo," replied Luther defensively.

Paine snorted, a slight growl to his muzzle. "*I* don't."

"That's why I don't take you. There was one time"— he resumed addressing Miranda even as they pressed against the wall like spies—"where he tried to open the timber wolf cage, and even though I talked him out of it I still got blamed when they found us there together...we almost got thrown out of the zoo!"

Luther sighed in disappointment even as Paine's ears pinned back.

"They're war criminals, keeping us locked up like that."

"Actually, proper zoos are vital for the conservation, breeding, and funding of endangered animals. The problem is that all too few zoos are proper...hold on." Miranda paused to listen to something, her large eyes narrowed with deep intent. "Who else is down here?"

When her whisper faded, Luther heard it.

"—told me you could pick locks, Dingus."

"I thought I could!" While Miranda edged to the corner of the hall, Luther almost jumped out of his skin.

"Pst! Miranda, come back! That's—"

"Ha-choo!"

Miranda and Luther's heads both whipped toward the great black wolf, who sniffled and wiped the tip of his nose with the back of one massive paw.

"Sorry," he said sheepishly, "allergies...it's sure dusty down here."

Around the corner of the hallway, one of the bullies asked, "You guys hear something?"

"We gotta go." Luther rushed to Miranda's side and grabbed one delicate hand. His skin burned on the contact. She glanced back, though her expression remained inscrutable. Trying to sound brave, he told her, "That's Brock Fliebolt, he's an asshole."

"So am I," answered Miranda, who proved immovable despite her delicate frame.

Shocked when his efforts to pull her away failed, Luther dropped her wrist and grit his teeth.

Well…if she wasn't going to run, he sure as heck couldn't. How would that look? Not just to her, but to Brock, and his toadies—even to Paine?

Sighing, the boy squared his shoulders and prepared to be punched in the face at some point in the next few minutes.

The bullies rounded the corner and almost careened right into them.

"Oh! It's just Weirdass Watson. Is this your girlfriend, Weirdass? Looks like it." While Brock sneered over his shoulder at his giggling toadies, Luther and his friends all exchanged wry looks. Even disguised as a stuffed animal, Paine seemed to roll his eyes.

"What's wrong with having a girlfriend?"

Miranda's question caught the bully off-guard, as though he had forgotten that girls could speak…or speak to him.

"What's wrong? What's wrong is that Watson's a freak, so you must be a freak, too."

"I'd say it's more normal to have a girlfriend than to pick on somebody for having one. Are you jealous? Luther didn't tell me you had a crush on him."

His prematurely acned face flushing with humiliation, Brock blustered around for a few seconds before coming up with the age-old comeback of the stupid: "What's that supposed to mean?"

"Nothing. Only that we would have been more subtle, so as to avoid hurting your feelings. He should have told me his bully was gay."

While the toadies barked out a few laughs of surprise, Brock whipped around and clocked Nick right in the gut. While the boy doubled over, the bully turned back to Miranda and raised his fist.

"Say I'm a homo again."

"There's nothing wrong with being gay," she assured him. "It's perfectly normal. I just didn't realize, that's all."

The bully cocked back his fist.

Luther cried out, already leaping between them.

Miranda didn't move.

The bully's fist stopped centimeters short of her nose, his expression strange after failing to make the girl flinch.

His pupils shrank.

Was he afraid of her?

"Like I said." The boy lowered his hand and snorted lightly. He looked Miranda over before glancing over his shoulder at his cohorts. "Total freak."

One of them snickered, about to make some pathetic response, when a door hidden by the corner opened. Somebody called, "Excuse me!"

Helpless in the face of adult responsibility, bullies and bullied all froze alike...except, of course, for Miranda, who turned her blasé expression toward the supposed stuffed animal in her friend's arms.

Roger, the guy whose office was their first stop, came around the corner with the weird, overbearing air of an adult about to tell off a group of kids he didn't know.

"Are you with one of the classes upstairs?"

"Yes," answered Miranda on their behalf. "We're sorry. We got lost looking for the shadow room."

Roger's somewhat annoyed affect relaxed marginally. Clearly this was a lie he was willing to believe because it was easier than disciplining a bunch of strangers. "Well this is the staff area, so try not to wind up down here again. Why don't you follow me? I'll show you right to it."

Amazingly, Brock flicked Miranda something resembling a look of respect.

Not even noticing, Miranda turned right around and led the way to the stairs.

As they were shepherded after her by Roger, Luther breathed a sigh of relief. All right! Now that they'd been caught, that would be that. He'd never been so glad to bump into Brock.

Unfortunately, nothing worked out so easily.

Upstairs, as Roger left the grudging kids by the shadow room, one of the teachers called to him from a swarm of students. "Have fun, guys," he said with a wave to the group he'd accompanied back to the public area, leaving them without a second thought— especially as he paused halfway to his destination.

"Excuse me! That exhibit—that's out of service, please get off of that—"

As a few giggling first-graders sprang off the dismantled exhibit that was piled up in indiscernible parts behind a line of CAUTION tape, Brock sniffed, re-assessed Miranda for a few seconds, then jutted his chin in a nod.

Miranda nodded in response, her large eyes lidded with disinterest.

"Let's get out of here," muttered the bully, ducking away with his pals and heading into the main exhibit hall.

Saying nothing, Miranda grabbed Luther's wrist before he could even relax.

"Miranda," he hissed as she marched him right back the way they'd come, "Miranda, what are you doing!"

"Now's our chance. Did you see? Roger left his office door open."

While Luther's stomach sank, Miranda pushed open the stairwell door and shoved him in.

On the other side, Paine no longer pretended to be a stuffed animal. "If anybody's going to have spare keys to this place," the wolf said with a sage nod as they hurried down the stairs, "it's going to be that guy."

"I guess so," Luther agreed, his tone somewhat miserable. "I just can't help but think the pay-off isn't going to be worth the risk."

"On the contrary. It will give you social credit." Releasing the boy's flushed wrist but still maintaining a somewhat brisk stride, Miranda led the way back along the hall and to Roger's open office. "If you get the scoop on the janitor to this place, everybody will think you're cool and interesting and a little bit edgy. It will impress them, just like having a girlfriend. If you play your cards right, Luther, you may be bullied quite a lot less after today."

The boy's cheeks flushed, not just at the thought of having a girlfriend but at the possibility Miranda presented.

He really could use a break from the constant torment.

"All right," he agreed, nodding and sighing as he did. "I'll do it."

Paine shook his head. "I'm telling you, Luther...it would be a lot simpler if you'd just let me kill them."

Luther shot him a sharp, grim look until Miranda uttered an unexpected laugh. "Yes, it would be simpler," she agreed with a nod, pushing Roger's door open just a little wider. "But where's the fun in it?"

Though Paine strolled right in, Luther hesitated on the edge of the office. It seemed like the last and greatest transgression in an increasing sequence of them. *Would* it be the last? He sure hoped...but he guessed not, if they were going to at least make it to the janitor's office and whatever secret it contained.

"Come in," she urged him, peering around the

cluttered space where wall-mounted shelves overflowed with books stacked on top of one another, and the wall calendar was set to the month prior, and the science DVDs littering the installed bookshelves seemed to mostly be from about fourteen years before either one of them had been born. Textbooks and action figures (a cool little mecha of some kind, for instance) littered the desk, and no inbox was visible beneath the pile of documents that had outgrown it.

Intrigued, Luther picked up the mecha only to have Miranda take it out of his hands.

"Look for the keys," she urged him. "Paine, listen for us. If somebody comes in, let's hide."

The boy almost laughed at that. "Where?"

Tapping her chin, Miranda looked around the room, then glided to the slatted door of a closet Luther had barely noticed amid all the clutter. She threw it open, turned on the light, then paused.

"What..."

While Luther's attention was caught by her curiosity, Paine noticed a golf bag and its accompanied clubs leaning in the corner of the office. Smiling, the wolf hurried over to it and slid the putter out to give it a test.

"You can tell just as soon as looking at this office that this guy is disorganized and lazy," said the wolf with a judgmental shake of his head. "I mean, come on! Bringing golf clubs to work? He's planning to leave early today."

"Or give a physics demonstration," Miranda said wryly. "But I suspect he is more interested in metaphysics at the given moment. See?"

While Luther hurried over at the wave of her hand, Miranda slipped to the back of the closet and moved aside a piles of old coats and office supplies. When she had revealed the tub of mushrooms, she explained, "A strain of *Psilocybe cubensis* known as "golden teachers." A popular and easy-to-grow strain of psychedelic mushroom."

When the young boy stared blankly at her, Miranda rolled her eyes.

"They're drugs," she explained. "They expand your mind, they're what hippies do. Apparently, whatever the janitor is up to, he wasn't the only one up to no good."

"Sounds pretty good to me," Paine remarked with a chuckle, sliding out a different club and now pawing around the side of the bag for a ball. Finding one with a grin, the wolf aimed for the nearest wastepaper basket. "Mushrooms can treat depression, anxiety, all kinds of mental illness— Sh!"

Hushing himself, the wolf paused before he could tap the ball. His fur bristled.

From the far distance of the hallway's end, Roger could be heard whispering too indistinctly to be understood.

"Hide," urged the wolf, scooping the golf ball back up and sliding the club into the bag.

Grimacing at the compromised exit, Luther ducked into the closet with Miranda. Paine slipped in and shut the door.

Just as the closet clicked shut, the office door swung open.

7

ROGER WAS JUST too high for any of this.

The problem with microdosing was that it was a fine line between 'micro' and 'macro' when you were talking about psychedelics—especially mushrooms, which could vary in potency depending on the amount of water they contained, the length of time they were grown before being picked, and even the strain or environment you were talking about growing them in.

And Roger, who had been experimenting with growing and consuming the things for about two years now, had evidently developed a fairly potent growing method.

A little too potent, one might say.

He felt the bad vibes coming on while he was talking to that creepy old janitor. Maybe it was just the janitor himself, or the act of having to fire him... but Roger hadn't wanted to blame the mushrooms. Certainly not at first.

After a certain point, though, it became evident that the mouthful of mushroom flesh he'd consumed that morning may have been a little beyond the threshold of a microdose. He could still function and was fairly confident nobody was onto him. If they thought something was up, they would never think to suspect psychedelic mushrooms, anyway.

Maybe.

But what if they *did?*

The paranoia was intense, the mushrooms were making it feel like needles prickled all over his flesh, and he had begun to think incessantly about the earliest possible moment he could sneak out for the day.

Damn. He had been planning for a nice afternoon at the golf course, lightly mellowed from the microdose and three quarters of a day at work. Now he was going to have to go home and lie down in the tub for a couple of hours to sort through whatever existential crisis the mushroom was about to give him.

The last thing he wanted was to bump into Deborah Carraway in this condition, which was exactly what happened...mostly because she was looking for him.

He had emerged with the group of lost kids and

dropped them off, intending to talk to the front desk people to let them know he was under the weather and taking the rest of the day off. Then, Deborah had caught his eye and waved him over to ask some stupid question. Something about cleaning supplies in the case of emergency.

He knew what she wanted, and normally the idea was naughty and fun...but he couldn't have been less in the mood if he tried.

"I don't know if now is a great time for this, Deborah," he murmured to her in the stairwell as they slipped away together, the artifice of their trip to the closet disappearing as soon as they were alone. "I'm pretty beat today, and I've still got a lot to do before I'm able to sneak out of here."

This was a lie—he could sneak out any time he wanted—but the only way to shake her off would be pretending to have things to do.

Not today.

Pouting in an objectively annoying way that she always seemed to think was irresistible, Deborah pressed her tight body to his side and contorted her eyebrows. "But I haven't gotten a chance to be with you in *weeks*, Roger! Don't you like me anymore?"

It wasn't that, of course, so much as that he was living in the semi-permanent visionary state of a Siberian mystic. All the same, he comforted his mistress while she slid against his body.

"Of course I like you," he assured her, sighing as her

hand slid over the front of his trousers. Well, he was hornier than he thought he'd be...but between the tour going on upstairs and the mushrooms threatening to freak him out, he really didn't have time or inclination to risk on a liaison.

"Tell you what," he said, guiding her down the hall and around the corner, "how about you and I take a few minutes in my office?"

Had he left the door open? Usually he was good about closing it when he left...damn kids, distracting him.

Ah...what was he blaming the kids for? They were just being kids. It was his own fault. The mushrooms' fault, too, if you wanted to get technical.

"I think you've been avoiding me," Deborah accused, sliding into the leather seat of the desk and propping her chin upon her fist to regard him. "First you canceled our date at the movies, now you're making up reasons to turn me down when I'm right here in front of you!"

"And when we're both at work," said Roger with a sigh. "I have a career to maintain, you know."

"And so do I! But passion doesn't wait for the sake of career. I want you now, Roger."

Deborah leaned against the desk and let her crimson hair tumble around her face, her red lip bitten all the while. With serpentine sensuality, she slid upon the desk and knelt there. Her body swayed to some unheard rhythm.

"Don't you want to touch me, Roger?"

Her hand glided over the short green sweater she used to cover the straps of her pink dress. One dropped away, unveiling the splash of freckles he loved to kiss along the beautiful line of her shoulder.

He couldn't resist anymore.

As she sighed, "Walter never touches me these days," Roger slid up behind her with his hands fitting to her shoulder blades from the first second of contact.

"You know I hate it when you talk about him," said Roger between kisses down the column of her neck, his nose buried in the rich perfume of her hair. "Don't talk—let's not talk at all."

While Deborah sighed, Roger reached around to cup one plentiful breast.

The coat closet shuffled.

Roger's entire career flashed before his eyes.

Was he just hearing things? That had certainly seemed to him like a crisp, clear, very real sound. Something being knocked or moved. Pale, he lurched away from Deborah.

"Did you hear that?"

"What?" Her tone was flat with annoyance as she turned to face him, but he was already on his way to the gasping closet.

Each step, he prepared himself. Whatever Roger was going to find—a student, a teacher, even a parent volunteer—it was going to be bad for his reputation. Everything he'd worked for would be destroyed if he didn't find some way to handle this elegantly.

How he phrased his speech would depend on who he found spying on him, so he wasted no time in throwing open the door.

He just wasn't expecting that he'd have to explain it all to a wolf.

8

MIRANDA HAD ALREADY taken quite a shine to Luther and Paine, but nothing touched that moment when the science museum director opened the closet door.

Oh, it had been funny (and interesting) before then. Luther, gravely embarrassed, had slapped one hand over his own eyes and stood on his toes in an effort to cover Paine's. With a wagging tail and ears perked in interest, Paine had simply pushed the small human's hand away while flashing a grin as if the real funny part were harassing Luther, which, of course, was the case.

Sex wasn't very interesting. It was too basic. What Miranda found interesting was the dysfunction of adults who still continued to have sex even though they didn't like one another.

Why bother? Especially when you weren't even married. It was, so far as she was concerned, the closest thing to funny outside the Zapruder Film. Like some kind of inside joke. Every set of parents she had met outside her own suffocatingly, grossly interwoven ones had seemed to only barely avoid trying to kill one another.

Irritated with Paine's attempts to avoid being sheltered, Luther gritted his teeth and did something so stupid that Miranda had to close her eyes for a few seconds.

He hopped up toward the wolf's height to more effectively cover his eyes.

When the movement bumped the wolf back against a rack of rolled posters, the director's head whipped their way.

By the time Miranda had recovered her senses and opened her eyes, the urge to strangle the boy she liked having faded, Roger pulled the door open.

And his eyes fixed on the big, black wolf.

His gigantic pupils froze, twitched, then rolled up into his head as he collapsed right on the spot.

"Roger!"

Shrieking, Mrs. Carraway—*Mrs.* Carraway, mind you—leapt up from the desk and rushed to the closet. She paused midway, her face contorting with anger to recognize Miranda within.

"Miranda Even, what the hell are you doing in there?"

"You shouldn't swear, Mrs. Carraway…or sleep with men who aren't your husband."

"Get out of the way! Oh, Roger—what's happened?"

"He was taking magic mushrooms," said the girl, stepping out of the closet and gesturing in. Luther, head down, scrambled with her. "Forgive me—'has been' taking magic mushrooms. He's not dead…just looks like it."

"How do you know what—oh, never mind. More, like how *could* you know he's taking anything?"

"Just a guess."

Mrs. Carraway followed Miranda's pointed finger in a skeptical rage, only to balk at the aquarium of mushrooms carefully tended with a timed light, a humid environment and several little pillars of vermiculite. Fixing the strap of her dress, Mrs. Carraway flipped on the closet light and bent to investigate.

And, while Miranda dragged Mr. Garnet's feet out of the way, Paine slammed the closet door shut.

"Hey!"

Mrs. Carraway and Luther uttered the objection at the same time, the boy's fearful eyes wild as they whipped between his two more mischievous friends. While the wolf effortlessly held the door shut, Miranda bent to unclip the key ring from the museum director's belt.

"I don't think anyone will find you anytime soon," advised Miranda, locking the closet door handle that uselessly jiggled against the wolf's weight. "But, if they do, I would also advise you to remember that we saw you two doing things that were extremely inappropriate, in the middle of a school day, during a field trip to a children's science museum."

"Let me *out* of here, you—this isn't a funny joke—"

"You don't have to pretend you feel anything toward me but a vague sense of unease, Mrs. Carraway," said Miranda, looking around the room in thought. She nodded at a big metal cabinet that looked like it had office supplies. "See if there's duct tape in there."

"Duct tape—"

"You could get in very serious trouble for this, Miranda—no, change that. You *both will* be in serious trouble for this when Roger wakes up or I've been found."

"That's why we're going to make it harder for you to help one another."

After plucking Mr. Garnet's keys and phone from his pocket, as well as fetching Mrs. Carraway's phone from her abandoned sweater, Miranda dropped both into the black pockets of her dress and unplugged the landline on the desk. While Mrs. Carraway protested, Miranda cut its cords into pieces with a depressingly blunt pair of scissors.

"Between you and me, Mrs. Carraway, I'm not sure you're meant for teaching. You need a lot of patience to deal with children...and you have to be smarter than they are."

Letting the wires fall at her feet, Miranda bent to remove Mr. Garnet's tie to form a gag for him. All the while, she asked Mrs. Carraway, "Do you really think that you're smarter than me?"

"You—you're a fucked-up, creepy, weird little psycho!"

While Miranda laughed at one of Mrs. Carraway's remarks for the first time ever, she tied the gag around the back of Mr. Garnet's head.

"Takes one to know one," she said, leaning back to examine the start of her work.

Clenching her teeth, eyes blazing beneath her wild hair, Mrs. Carraway took a great breath.

"Hel—"

Paine turned the nearby AM/FM radio on at full blast as soon as reluctant Luther pulled a roll of duct tape from the cabinet.

Above the inundation of Mariachi music, Luther asked, "Is this really necessary?"

"We've just locked my teacher in a closet and non-consensually borrowed—"

"Stolen," substituted Paine.

"—the keys of the wayward museum director," she said with a gesture down at the supine man. "You don't want me to get into trouble, do you, Luther?"

"We'll get into even *more* trouble if we tie this guy up."

"No, we won't."

"Of course we will!"

"I'm telling you, we won't."

"How can you possibly think that?"

"Because. I never get in trouble."

The boy produced a short little laugh, pausing and folding his arms over his chest. "Yeah, bet you'll think that until this afternoon."

"It's true. You wanted to know about me, right? My 'thing,' as you called it before?" Standing and dusting off her hands, Miranda shrugged. "I'm smart, but many people are smart. I like strange things, but many people are strange. My 'thing' is that no matter what I do, I end up avoiding responsibility...even when people know I was the one who did it. The times that I do get into trouble, it always amounts to nothing."

Eyes flashing, Miranda asked, "Would you like to know how?"

Heaving a great sigh, Luther extended the duct tape to the girl.

Miranda shook her head.

"First, we have to rearrange some furniture."

After a few minutes of coordinated efforts between the students and the wolf—all of whom, it goes without saying, ignored the pleas, promises and demands of the captured teacher—the set had been rearranged. Roger's desk had been moved in front of the shut closet, just in case the slats or low quality of the door permitted it to yield to Mrs. Carraway's occasional shoves.

Roger, for his part, had been dragged up into his

chair and strapped in with the duct tape. It sort of amazed Miranda that he didn't wake up with all the jostling and dragging, but she supposed the human mind really required a huge reboot when, as an adult in one's forties, one saw their first inter-dimensional entity with no warning.

"I can't believe *he* saw Paine, too," muttered the boy under his breath. With loud music playing on the radio and Mrs. Carraway still bitterly complaining in the closet, Miranda shut the door to Roger's office and locked it with his keys.

"Probably just the drugs," she explained.

"I know that," said Luther as he followed her to the stairs, amending, "well, or at least, that makes sense, but it's just—my whole life, nobody's ever seen him but me. Not *really* seen him, anyway."

"Somebody's got to see him sometime, right?" Miranda shrugged. "Maybe it's just time. Or maybe it's like that old saying, you know...the horses are out of the barn."

"Yeah," said Luther, "or cat's out of the bag."

"Cat? Where!"

Barking, howling, Paine whipped his head around and rushed down the hallway.

Brow knitting in panic, Luther cried, "Wait, Paine!"

Though Miranda protested, the boy was already chasing his friend.

Sighing with displeasure, she hurried after them both.

It was true she had been planning to go back upstairs, since that was the most likely place for the janitor's office. Aside from needing such a figure frequently and instantly in a children's museum, janitors tended to have all manner of tools that were meant to be rolled, dragged, or were otherwise too cumbersome to carry up a flight of stairs.

It therefore seemed that the most logical place to find the treasure she sought was in the first floor. Near the bathrooms, perhaps? She hadn't seen anything like that and had known they would investigate.

Miranda had, however, wanted to run the investigation stealthily. She certainly hadn't wanted to bump into Luther's girl-friends; and she certainly hadn't wanted those girls to see Luther instantly, their eyes wide as they emerged from the exhibit hall and scanned the area.

While the shutting stairwell door latched behind them and Luther looked hurriedly around for the wolf who was nowhere to be seen, one of the girls cupped her hands around her mouth.

"Luther! Hey, Luther, we're over here!"

Head sharply turning their way, Luther caught sight of the girls in the crowd. His expression flatlined.

"I should go talk to them," he said, only glancing over once when he realized Miranda was following him. "Uh—are you sure you want to come?"

"I don't mind."

"They're really rude girls."

"Do they like you?"

Luther sputtered, his voice rising in embarrassment. "Why does everybody keep asking me that?"

"Asking what?"

While two girls of the group meandered over to the pneumatic ping-pong ball track in the lobby, one girl popped up before Luther. Wanting to be polite, Miranda focused on the pair tinkering with the toy. One of the girls took her turn pumping up the pressure of the machine so that, when released, the ping-pong ball within would whizz up, through the track all around the ceiling of the lobby, then roll back down into its customary cradle.

Luther, still stuttering a little as he recovered his senses, shook his head at the interloper's question. "Nothing, never mind. Are you—uh, having fun, Stacy?"

"God, you're acting so weird, Luther...who's this?"

"Oh, uh—"

Looking awkwardly over at Miranda, Luther searched her expression for some help but found none. Not having yet determined whether this girl was a bully or a friend, she waited. Upon wiping his palms across his shirt, Luther said, "This is my, uh, my...girlfriend."

Miranda's heart felt like it was beating for a second. The air seemed clearer and fresher in her lungs.

As the ping-pong ball followed its natural course through the track, this 'Stacy' girl's face went from annoyed and expectant to annoyed and confused and just a little mad.

"Your *girlfriend*," she repeated, looking between them. "Oh, really!"

"Yeah," said Luther, the confirmation coming more boldly than Miranda would have expected it to. "Yeah, that's her."

"I didn't know you had a girlfriend."

Miranda looked at her blankly. "Did you ever ask?"

With an annoyed wrinkle of her nose, the girl decided she was better off ignoring Miranda's existence altogether. Grabbing Luther's wrist, she demanded, "Well, that's great, but we have to finish our assignment. Come on."

"Actually, uh—"

Luther pulled himself from the girl's grip and told her with an increasing confidence, "I already finished the group assignment...I forgot that my parents took me here this summer."

Her tone withering, the girl looked between them again. "Oh, really."

"Yeah, so...I filled the worksheet out and gave it to Mrs. Johnson, and she said we can go play until lunch."

"Gotcha," said the girl in a bitchy tone. "Must be nice. Well, have fun!"

Flipping one pigtail over her shoulder as Luther said, "Hey, but Stacy, wait," she ignored any further sound from him and flounced off to join her friends.

Luther watched her go with a sigh.

"So you *do* like her," decided Miranda, earning a glance from the boy.

"I mean, I guess she's pretty, but she's really mean to me and I'm pretty mean to her, too. And, anyway...I only thought she was pretty because I'd never seen you before."

To hide the strange impulse to smile, Miranda looked around the bustling museum and changed the subject. "Look for a door that's intentionally nondescript."

"Don't you think we should find Paine?"

"Isn't he a grown-up wolf?"

"Well, yes, but—"

"Then he can take care of himself. Come on."

Miranda reached back for his hand and, holding it with their fingers interwoven, she led Luther around the wall of the museum. "Try to look like we're looking for someone, rather than some*thing*."

Luther nodded to himself. "That's easy enough...I *am* looking for someone."

"You really worry about him, huh?"

"You don't know how out of control he gets," said Luther grimly. "Especially when he hasn't eaten in a few hours."

"Has he ever eaten anybody?"

Luther glanced at Miranda in the kind of quiet that was a long consideration as much as a tacit confirmation. Instead of answering with words, he answered with his subject change.

"What about you? What's the real reason everybody's so scared of you?"

"Lots of reasons."

"Name a real one."

Hadn't she already? Maybe a half-truth. As she glanced past an auditorium where a teacher rounded up some of the younger class members, Miranda decided to tell him, "I'm a performance artist. Mommy and Daddy say they don't understand performance artists in America these days."

"What kind of artist is a performance artist?"

"Well, like the last time I almost got into trouble but didn't, it was for playing a game called "Spanish Inquisition." It's very fun, and at the same time it teaches a lesson."

Luther's nose wrinkled. "That sounds boring. Who wants to learn a lesson from a game?"

"All games teach lessons...you just don't realize what the good ones are teaching you."

While they peered into some sort of a workshop where, on the other side of big glass windows, students scribbled the answers to worksheet questions or fooled around with magnetic boards that permitted the assembly of various gears used to turn a crank. In the back of the room, a few students milled around the glass-enclosed beehive mounted in the wall: hundreds, maybe thousands of the little black-and-yellow insects wiggled through their honeycomb maze and out of the museum altogether where the children could watch safely.

"I guess performance art's not so bad," said Luther at last, sounding decisive. "My parents get mad at me all the time for what I do with my snowmen—hey, look!"

With a more dynamic tug of the hand than she had come to expect from him, Luther jerked his head toward the electricity-generating bicycle.

Though the doorway behind it was open, the hallway had been blocked off by a gigantic cardboard cutout declaring "SCIENCE IS COOL!" with the help of a few stock photo kids in chemistry goggles.

Just behind one of their shoulders, Miranda spotted a door handle.

"Good eye," she said, genuinely impressed.

While Luther grinned at her in pride, his eye was snagged by something else. For a few seconds he boggled, whisper-shouting, "Hey!"

Miranda looked over her shoulder. Across the lobby, Paine tapped on the back of the pneumatic tube where the ping-pong ball was being pressurized. Ears twitching at the sound of his friend's voice, the wolf turned with an innocent grin and a wave of his paw.

"He's fine," said Miranda, who nodded to a pair of teachers conversing by the gift shop. "Let's go while they're not looking."

Huffing in slight annoyance, Luther nonetheless obeyed and moved along with Miranda. Their heads low, they passed the bike and darted around the cardboard cut-out.

As Luther moved their obstacle, Miranda fished for Roger's keys and searched through the ring for likely suspects. Only three seemed of the same material as the shiny chrome lock before them, and when Miranda tried the second key, everything was rewarded.

The tumbler clicked beneath the key; the door to the janitor's office swung wide.

Though disappointing at first glance, the room held a certain air of mystery. The janitor's name, "C. KRUMB," remained upon the brass nameplate sitting at the front edge of his desk. To the old man's credit, it was a far tidier desk than Roger's.

The rest of the room, however, needed work.

While Luther hurried in and shut the door after them, Miranda struggled to discern cleaning supplies from clutter. An old television had been piled upon yellowed newspapers, as though to make it easier for someone sitting at the desk to watch it without straining their neck. No windows meant that the dim fluorescent lights leant a sickly hue to everything, including the children.

And at first glance, as she had anticipated, nothing was amiss.

"That was anticlimactic," quipped Luther.

Doing a slow pass around the perimeter of the room, Miranda studied the walls, the cabinets, and the piles of miscellaneous supplies ranging from bleach to turpentine.

"You can't expect whatever it is he's been hiding to be out in plain sight...or easily accessible."

"I don't know. If he's really got something as bad as illegal drugs growing in the closet like the guy in the basement"—what a puritan Luther was! he'd grow out of it, almost certainly—"then he'd better hope he hid it better than sticking it in a closet."

"This whole place is a janitor's closet," answered Miranda wryly, running her fingers along the wall and knocking in search of a hollow spot. "It's just a question of how much he was able to customize it while working here...and however untrustworthy they found him, he must have taught them a lesson for future janitors. That door only locks from the outside. They're probably planning to turn it into a real storage space...be sure to listen closely, Luther."

After completing her investigation and finding herself back at the door, Miranda made one more visual sweep. Then, she worked on the desk. With no locks, it was easy to search as it was fruitless.

"Not even a dirty magazine," she said to herself.

"What could he have been hiding, then? Maybe you misunderstood."

"I know what I heard," Miranda said simply, glancing over the cluttered floor and then across the ceiling. "The desperation in his tone, the way he threatened to tell Mr. Garent's secrets...Krumb's got something to protect."

At last, she noticed it.

One of the tiles was just a little crooked.

"Help me set up this ladder," said Miranda, waving him over.

Soon, with the ladder arranged and stabilized thanks to Luther's support, Miranda balanced upon the second highest rung. Her tongue set against her teeth, she leaned up and was pleased when her fingers just touched the nearest drop ceiling panel. She was getting taller.

"Good," she said, more to herself than to him. "I don't think we'll need the phone books after all."

Slowly, her heart close to racing with the anticipation of some macabre discovery, Miranda pushed at the tile.

"Are you sure this is a good idea?"

Miranda snorted a little at his question, freeing the tile and, because she swayed, jamming her foot against the rung where she stood.

"No wonder Paine ran ahead of us," she said, feeling atop the remaining tiles and idly hoping a spider would crawl over her hand so she could see if it was worth taking home. "You really do have a way of bringing down the mood by asking obvious questions..."

"Sorry."

His apology really did make her laugh, but the laughter was cut short when the tips of her fingers made contact with some kind of bag. Nylon? Felt like it. A gym bag.

Full of something hard.

"There's something up here," Miranda called down to her friend. "Keep me steady a few more seconds, then be ready to reach up and catch this thing... whatever it is, it feels hard enough to hurt you if you mess up."

"Wh—okay."

Though his tone was uneasy, Luther did as she'd asked and stretched his arms high at just the right moment. The bag was nearly too heavy for her to drag, and when the boy caught it he almost immediately dropped it.

But the important thing was that they got it down.

While it fell with a dangerous-sounding *clang*, Miranda made her way back down.

"Don't open it yet," she urged him. "Let's do it together."

"It does feel like finding some kind of lost treasure," remarked the boy. "What do you think it'll be? Gold?"

Miranda furrowed her brow sympathetically, patting his hand. Luther was so innocent! "Trust me—when adults have something like gold, they don't usually keep it secret."

Luther's expression grew grim as he studied the bag. "Jeez. Well, then...do we really want to know?"

"We've come so far now. Who could live without knowing?"

Shrugging, Miranda grabbed the zipper and pulled.

As Luther pushed aside the fabric to reveal the guns, she knew everything was worth it.

9

STACY TIFTON MAY have been a little spoiled. One would have been justified in calling her rude. 'Snotty,' on a very bad day.

And these were undesirable traits, there was no denying. Even Stacy had a few moments of self-awareness that made her think someday it might be good to change....but not right now. No matter how you looked at it, it was her parents' fault that she was turning out this way. If they wanted her to act differently now, they needed to assert some boundaries.

Besides—she may have been entitled to the enjoyment of a few more privileges than the average girl her age, but she wasn't *bad*. And she certainly wasn't a weirdo like that witchy girl Luther was apparently seeing.

What gave? The more Stacy thought about that claim, the smellier it got. Something here was wrong.

First of all...dating Luther?

Gross.

Super, mega gross.

Like, sure. He would be cute if you took a way that freaking loser stuffed animal of his. That would be one thing for sure. Then maybe he would sustain eye contact for more than twenty seconds before his blue eyes would dart away and off into the middle of nowhere.

What was that word everybody used? Autistic. She was starting to think Luther was autistic, which was lame, because if so it took all the joy out of teasing him. Besides, like she said—if he could just get over his...weirdness...he would come off like a really normal boy! Even a likable boy.

Even a dateable boy, in high school, maybe...after he had been given a few years of probation from Whatever Jail to reintegrate into normal society.

And anyway, Luther liked to put on this routine of being a pariah, but Stacy had been the recipient of shins kicked under the lunch table (even if she started it); and she had taken the blame for at least one burst paper bag (that resulted in her staying after lunch to clean the tables, thanks Luther); and whenever she deigned to invite Luther to play, he always messed it up (by wanting to incorporate his stupid, weird stuffed animal, which was just so embarrassing).

Really and truly, Stacy had *tried* to be nice to Luther. She always had—even back in Kindergarten, when he was the one who picked on her.

But in the matter of 'Paine,' (which was *such* a weird and disturbing name for a stuffed animal), there could be no compromise anymore. Stacy's tolerance for Paine had been a lot higher before he started coming to school every day, and all extra-curricular activities, and, yes, even field trips. She even saw him hauling the thing around the mall with his Mom one time.

Stacy just wasn't sure what had happened; but whatever the reason, Luther's need to carry around the stuffed toy was weird. On the elementary school playground, weirdness was the kiss of death. It was the ultimate sin for any student hoping to have a social life. The very second you revealed yourself as 'other' in even the slightest way, you risked total social alienation.

That was what Luther didn't understand, and what Stacy did. Social behavior was a *skill*. Nobody learned how to be social by being themselves all the time. You had to try to be like other people, and to try to be like other people you first had to get to know other people.

The only person Luther wanted to know was his stupid stuffed animal.

Stacy had plenty of stuffed animals of her own. She wasn't alienated by the concept of loving inanimate objects. It was just—the elaborate mythos that had been built around this toy in the confines of Luther's mind was really freaking sad.

So far as she could tell, he spent every waking minute thinking about this stuffed wolf. If he wasn't autistic then he was definitely OCD. That was obsessive personality stuff, like brushing your teeth twenty times for no reason other than because you were afraid of what would happen if you didn't. Consulting the wolf for its opinions and acting based on those opinions? Definitely had to qualify.

So, was Stacy *jealous* that this weirdo kid had a girlfriend? Of course not. As previously stated, she was not jealous at all, in any way.

However...her not-jealousy aside, this was all very concerning.

If Luther really did get a girlfriend while being a notorious weirdo, that meant his girlfriend was probably a weirdo, too. Didn't that mean she would *keep* him weird? That, instead of growing up and learning to fit in, he would want to stay weird so as to maintain his relationship with this 'Miranda' girl?

It nagged at Stacy. Especially as, watching the two weirdos walk together from where she was obscured by the crowd flowing throughout the lobby, she grew sickened to see that they were holding hands.

Just how long had this been going on?

There had to be a way to put a stop to it. After seeing the two disappear together behind the cardboard background of the electrical bike, Stacy gathered her friends around her and told them, "I'm going to be a minute. Why don't you guys finish the assignment while I'm gone, so that way we can hang out until lunch?"

Exchanging a glance with Terra, Jessica said with only the most thinly veiled displeasure, "Where are *you* going?"

"That weirdo chick is Luther's girlfriend," said Stacy tersely. "I just saw them go someplace alone, and this may be my only opportunity to see if she realizes who she's dealing with."

"More like you're worried they're kissing in secret," giggled Jessica, laughing all the harder at Stacy's scowl.

"No way! I don't care about that. I'm just worried about her...she probably has no idea how bad his reputation is at our school since she's from one of the places around Smokeland."

"No wonder he was able to pull the wool over her eyes."

"Exactly. So, I have to do the right thing and warn her."

Ditching her friends with barely more than a wave before they could confirm or deny that they would solve the group problems without her, Stacy said, "I'll see you guys soon and let you know how it goes."

On the way to the cardboard cut-out, Stacy's stomach tied itself in knots.

What *if* they were kissing in there? It made

her sick to think of somebody she'd known since Kindergarten—somebody who could just grow up a little bit and be fine material for a first boyfriend for someone like Stacy—could just go...*kiss someone.* Someone *else.*

Holding back her barf, Stacy looked around to make sure no teachers were watching before she slipped past the bike and the cardboard barrier. There was no sign of Luther and that girl. Just a door, plus a squat little hallway that, when investigated, led out to the employee parking lot.

Stacy let the parking lot door swing shut. Just as she did, something loud clattered to the floor inside the shut room. Heart racing, her dread turning to relief, Stacy crept back to the door and pressed her ear against the poorly painted surface.

Inside, someone was rustling around with something. The two whispered together.

A zipper was pulled.

Stacy's stomach sank, especially as Luther asked with a sharp gasp and a strangled, strange sort of noise, "Is that—"

"Sh."

Luther fell silent at the strange girl's hush, but his breathing was so rapid that Stacy could hear it through the door.

Her eyes filled with tears.

How awful! Was this the sort of thing Luther wanted? And so *early!* It must have been this girl's influence. Poor Luther was running around with some harlot from another school, and as a result he was being initiated into a world of gross adult things that were way beyond anything anybody their age needed to know.

Don't ask Stacy how she knew they didn't need to know about them.

As their voices dropped to intense whispers and something inside could be heard clicking, Stacy's own shameful chiding from earlier rushed back to her. Hadn't she been the one telling Luther to grow up right to his face while they were waiting to get on the bus?

Well...maybe he *could* stand to be a kid for awhile longer. Maybe Paine wasn't so weird after all. Maybe it was weirder to try to pretend that you were an adult when in reality you were only nine years old.

Maybe Stacy really did like Luther, and the idea of someone from another school corrupting him made her want to cry.

She had to do something. She couldn't just stand there and let whatever was happening unfold without intervention.

Bracing herself for whatever she saw, a small price to pay in exchange for Luther's rescue, Stacy threw open the door.

Luther and the weird girl both turned, the assault rifles in their hands almost comically over-sized in comparison to their bodies.

Assault rifles?

"Stacy—"

Luther's utterance of her name went completely unheard as the components of the image settled into Stacy's brain. The door had swung shut behind her by the time it made any sense.

Assault rifles. Guns? Children with guns? Shooter. Shooters. School shooters?

Museum shooters.

Not knowing what else to do or make of the situation, Stacy opened her mouth to scream.

The bullet cracked right between her eyes.

10

LUTHER'S JAW DROPPED open at the same rate Stacy's body fell to the floor.

It was happening again.

While Luther stood, staring at the corpse in a state of paralysis, Miranda set down the rifle that had released an abrupt spray of three or maybe four bullets at her touch of the trigger.

"Teachers will be coming," said the girl, hurrying over to the corpse. "Help me move her out of the way so we can have a few extra seconds. I don't think we should kill them yet, though, so just point, don't fire. Help me!"

Luther snapped from his daze to realize Miranda held Stacy by the ankles. Grimly slinging the gun around his neck, Luther cringed before grabbing the dead girl's shoulders but forced himself to do what needed doing.

"Why did you do that," he hissed while they slid her along the concrete floor and into the corner of the room farthest from the door. "Why would you ever do that?"

Miranda shrugged. "She was about to scream. Teachers are going to come one way or another, but now we can control the situation."

"Wh—are you crazy? What are you talking about!"

"I mean, if somebody found us fooling around with guns, we would be in *real* trouble. Way more trouble than just breaking into the basement. And I already told you, Luther...I never get in *real* trouble."

Luther's eyes filled with tears. This girl was insane! Cute, maybe, but scarily insane. He was going to have to get away from her as soon as possible and get a teacher, or a parent supervisor, or something.

But, as she picked the gun back up, Luther was certain he had to play along with her at least until he could make good an escape.

Somebody knocked on the door of the janitor's office.

Was escape likely? Maybe not. The door opened and the teachers from his school, Mrs. Johnson and Ms. Viola, stepped into the room.

Seeing his own teacher was too much. Luther turned and puked uncomfortably near the corpse, the slowly expanding pool of blood that mingled into the chunks of orange barf inspiring a second wave as soon as his watering eyes were able to focus again.

"The gun, Luther," exclaimed Miranda, already pointing hers at the teachers who noticed her too late. "You—shut the door."

"What's going—oh, God!"

Ms. Viola's face contorted into an expression of wild-eyed horror. Much like Stacy's, however, her scream was halted by the lifting of Miranda's gun.

"Don't make me use this again. The first time was an accident; the second time never is. Shut the door."

On the second iteration of the grade schooler's command, Mrs. Johnson looked with shock and shame over at Luther.

When he averted his eyes, they did as they'd been told.

"This is a terrible mistake," said Mrs. Johnson solemnly.

Luther nodded, tears rolling down his cheeks. "I know."

"Don't listen to them, Luther. Keep pointing the gun."

He clenched his teeth, remembering that he had a part in all this, and reluctantly obeyed. Miranda let hers hang down, its strap around her shoulders with the gun upon her back like a knapsack.

"If either one of you makes a sound," she continued to the adults, "we're going to have to kill you."

"What reason could you two possibly have to hurt us—or poor Stacy?" Mrs. Johnson's eyes blazed with indignance behind the gloss of sorrow. "Oh, Stacy! Is there any chance she's still alive?"

"None. I don't miss."

"How *dare* you show so little regard for human—"

Mrs. Johnson gagged as Miranda flipped the rifle back around and slammed the butt into the old lady's stomach. As the teacher keeled over and Ms. Viola, crying out, fled down to her side, Miranda fetched old cleaning rags from the shelves.

"I would prefer not to treat you unkindly. If you'll cooperate, we can see what we can do for you." Miranda displayed the rags. "Otherwise, this may end up being much worse."

With a long, anxious, pleading look at Luther, who studied his shoes and wondered where Paine was, the teachers regarded one another.

Then, the cloths in Miranda's hand.

The next few minutes passed in a haze. At least all Luther had to do was stand there and try not to think about the fact that he was pointing a gun at two people. Soon, all four confiscated smartphones had been destroyed, the television played an old Western at high volume, and the teachers were gagged and bound—but not to Miranda's satisfaction.

"We're going to have to be back to check on them soon," she said, plucking the duct tape she'd applied over the cloth with a skeptical air. "This room is too full of tools to leave them alone in for very long…let's lock them in and come back once we've found a patsy."

"A patsy?"

"We need someone to blame," said Miranda plainly, shrugging her shoulders at the self-evident fact. "A person is dead and four others are about to be."

"Wh—who?"

"These two, and Mr. Garnet and my teacher, of course. We just have to figure out how we'll do it quietly."

Luther's eyes bugged in his head while Miranda slid the gun's strap off and gently lay the rifle back with its others. As she nodded in indication he should do the same, the teachers protested against their gags and Luther said, "I thought you were going to make things better for them, since they cooperated!"

"If you want to learn to get out of trouble, you have to be willing to tell anyone anything. Look, Luther—"

Miranda set a hand on his shoulder. Though he jumped, his eyes fixed on hers and remained there, mesmerized.

"All of this," she said with a wave, "is happening in a vacuum."

His mind reeled. "A vacuum?"

"Yes. A non-space, like a black hole. Have you ever heard the saying 'No body, no crime?'"

The phrase churned Luther's stomach. His eyes darted away from Miranda's, across their bound victims, and toward the door. "Uh-huh."

"That's what I mean. If we're not held accountable, we'd might as well have not done it."

"Do you ever get the feeling you're—I don't know... missing something, Miranda? Like, I don't know, what's the word...'empathy?'"

"I wouldn't say I'm missing it," the girl quipped in her usual deadpan tone, kneeling to zip the bag shut. "Now, when we go out there, we're going to have to act natural. As naturally as we can, anyway, carrying this duffle bag around."

"What if somebody stops us?"

"I'll say I was told to do a favor for Mrs. Carraway and bring supplies down to the basement."

Luther nodded slightly, his head aching with the second reality presented by the narrative of all the day's lies.

Miranda paused, one hand on the knob of the door.

"You know, Luther...for having just seen your first dead body, you're awfully calm."

Luther's lips pressed thin. He found himself once again unable to look at her.

"I don't mean it in a bad way. It's just that—"

"Can we just go."

Even he was surprised by the hard, simple tone of his voice. It got the message across, though.

Nodding, Miranda cracked open the door and slipped out before anyone in the excessively loud, sometimes giddily screaming lobby could notice the muffled noises of the teachers echoing from their discreet side hall.

After resisting the urge to look at them one last time, Luther followed her and watched her back as she locked the door behind them.

Obviously, none of this was the right thing to do. As soon as they had found a duffel bag of guns in the fired janitor's office, they should have reported it to a teacher or the director or somebody else who was a responsible adult. Their curiosity and Miranda's foolhardy insistence that it wasn't a problem were the primary causes of this grave into which they dug themselves.

But Miranda seemed to think that when you were in a grave you couldn't climb out of, you could just keep on digging until you came out in China.

And, well…much like last time, Luther would rather learn a whole new alphabet than let his parents think he was a murderer, or complicit in a murder.

Even if he was.

If anybody found out about Paine—*really* found out about him—it would be horrible. The wolf would be taken away and the boy would probably be—who knew? Luther shuddered. Every bad thing Paine ever did inevitably ended up blamed on him, after all… Luther didn't want to think about what would happen when he was finally pinned with something Big.

Maybe, if that was going to be the case, Luther needed a girlfriend who could never get into "real" trouble.

"I'm trusting you," said Luther under his breath to Miranda, who glanced over at him.

She reached out and caught his hand.

Even with the bag, they blended into the chaos of the museum in a state of perfect camouflage. Luther and Miranda were just two of many children: running in all directions; leaping off the pulley chair once they'd dragged themselves up as high as the model Rover; rushing to leaping on to the spirograph machine they would then ride like a surfboard; darting from one exhibit wing to another.

And, of course, screaming. Someone, somewhere, always screaming.

No wonder the gunfire was unrecognized by but a few eagle-eared adults in the wrong place at the wrong time.

The remaining chaperones, not as adept with parsing the chaos, were having an impossible time. Their searching eyes struck one another, each with a terrified glint that signaled the telepathic asking of a single desperate question: Where were the teachers?

Even the staff members of the museum seemed exhausted despite the cheer of their primary colored t-shirts, each wan face longing for a lunch hour that was surely minutes away. Luther hadn't seen a clock in forever, or at least hadn't been in a frame of mind to think about what time it was.

But now that he glanced around in hopes of finding one, all he saw was a bipedal wolf who speedwalked up with his front paws buried in his hip fur as though in human pockets.

"Hey guys! Fancy seeing you two here. What's crackin'?"

"We'll talk about it when we're all alone," answered Miranda without looking up as the wolf fell in with them, skulking along like a shadow while she guided them to their basement destination.

"Hey, that's cool, that's cool! I'll probably have something to talk about, too."

Luther looked sharply at his oldest friend. "Like what?"

Something cracked through the air: pinging, shattering, bouncing, careening.

A choir of voices, both young and old, screamed.

An intern in a red t-shirt intoning *SCIENCE IS COOL!* dropped dead in the middle of the lobby.

A golf ball had replaced the ping-pong ball in the pressurization device in the lobby, doing an untold amount of damage by smashing through the side of the tube before it could even reach the metal track. Propelled like an over-sized bullet of ultra-hard rubber coated in an even harder jacket, the ball bounced along the exterior of the track, pinged off at a sharp angle, bounced off the hook affixing the scale model Lunar Rover to the lobby's ceiling, and shot down straight into the intern's brain.

Paine would explain all that later, once the dust had settled.

For now, all anybody and everybody in the museum knew to be true was that something had made a loud cracking noise that came after other, previously dismissed cracking noises only heard by a scattered few; and that, as a consequence of this new cracking noise, one of the museum's interns dropped dead in full view of everyone in the lobby.

Half the children in the room who saw the collapse released a second wave of screams; the rest were already scrambling away.

Only an adult had frame of mind to shriek one word:

"Shooter!"

11

SHERIFF HAYWARD WASN'T sure what it was about that old janitor that sat crooked with him all morning long.

Here was the thing. You had to listen to every complaint, and, in a town this small, you had to follow *up* with every complaint. Otherwise, people'd talk and you'd lose your ass next election. It therefore behooved you to listen to a man, or t'act like you was.

And when a man told him something as serious as Krumb told Hayward, the Sheriff couldn't help but give it a long, hard think.

The problem was that Krumb had just been fired. Claude was known for being a real asshole all throughout the town of Smokeland—frankly, a borderline psychotic. His car was covered in writings that proclaimed the

CIA was trying to control the minds of citizens through cellphone technology, or some such. Said all kinds of things on there, probably. Sheriff Hayward hadn't bothered reading more than a word or two of it...if it didn't have the names Grisham or Sandford on the cover, he'd guarantee it wouldn't hold Hayward's attention for two damn seconds.

Anyway, the surly old man was not a very reliable source of information. He did not trust the police and had previously been a stubborn witness to consult on the crimes of others. Now that he had been fired from the science museum, it was mighty convenient this was the moment he chose to be forthcoming with any kind of information relating to any kind of crime.

That being said...allegations of *this* crime were very dangerous. Much like shouting 'fire' in a crowded theatre, it did not flatter the (alleged) criminal in trouble to point this type of finger. Not unless he wanted to stampede folk and slip town in the process.

So, Hayward gave the old janitor a little test to gauge his seriousness. If this was a real matter of concern, Krumb would be back the next day come rain or shine.

"I don't think you're *listening* to me, Sheriff!"

The old man had the small black eyes of a vole, his gaunt features shrunken and twisted from a lifetime of fighting with his missus, his bosses, and God, Himself. Now its every muscle quivered as though on the verge of an explosion similarly foretold by his blotching red skin.

"The man ain't just *planning* a shooting. He's got damn guns *in the museum!*"

"Then why the hell didn't you tell us this sooner?"

"Because I only found 'em last night! I couldn't decide what it meant until this morning—but before I could go in and use the phone, he stopped me at the door! Knew what I'd seen and fired me. Wanted me gone so he could do his bad business—must be he's planning something today."

"Do you have any evidence?"

"I saw 'em with my own two eyes!"

"Take a picture?"

"I don't have a damn cellphone!"

"Then why didn't you call us from your landline this morning, once you'd tossed and turned all night with this weighing on your conscience?"

The old man hesitated for only a second or two, but it was a second Sheriff Hayward noticed. He considered himself an expert in what was normal speech, and what was some very creative truth-telling. With Claude Krumb, he wasn't sure there was much difference.

"I didn't want to call from my house," the alleged witness said after the delay, "because I didn't want all this traced back to me in any way. You think I wanted to sit here today talking about any damn thing like this? No! But I had no other choice. Meeting you face-to-face was the only way to get you to listen."

"You tell your wife?"

"No one," answered the old man, leaning back in his seat and folding his arms across his thin chest.

Sighing, one heavily tanned hand of more brown than copper sweeping over his thinning hair, Sheriff Hayward said, "You know I'm gonna have to arrest you if I find you're lyin' to me, right, Claude?"

"I'm telling you, if you go look in my office—"

"*Your* office!"

"—up in the ceiling—"

"Now—now hold on, wait just a minute, now. What are you talkin' about, *your* office? He was hidin' guns up in the ceiling of *your* office?" Glancing at his lieutenant and leaning forward with a pen wiggling between his broad fingers, Sheriff Hayward folded his hands on the table and said, eyebrows steepling, "Now—why the hell would he go and do a thing like that?"

"Because he was planning to frame me, obviously."

"That right?"

"Yeah," said the bitter old man, his lips contorting in tight displeasure beneath the cop's stare. "That's right."

"And you're sure it's him, huh?"

"Ain't nobody else I know fucked up enough to grow psychedelic mushrooms in a children's science museum."

"Uh-huh. All right, well, I appreciate your information—"

"Now hold on a minute, I'm not—"

"But if we're gonna make a move on this information, I'd like to get things in motion to obtain a warrant as soon as I possibly can. How 'bout you let me work on my angle, and I'll have another sit-down with you tomorrow morning if you'd be so obligin' as to help us prepare for tomorrow's raid."

"It has to be *today*," insisted the old man. "What part of this are you not understanding?"

One or two things.

For instance...mass shooters were not frequently known for their desire to pin anything on anybody else. On the contrary, their very crimes were a desperate plea for attention.

And Sheriff Hayward, when confronted with these witch hunt-startin' words, could not helping but stop and ask himself who wanted attention more.

Did this Roger Garnet fella, a quiet city transplant who'd moved to Smokeland about four years prior, really need attention as bad as the fading old man with no kids, a sullen wife, and a job that had apparently decided it was time to put him out to pasture?

The answer was clear to him.

So, Sheriff Hayward did in fact turn right around and get a warrant.

But he got one for the residence of Mr. and Mrs. Claude Krumb.

To add a little to the stack of evidence, Hayward folded his arms after the muttering janitor was off city property. "Say, uh, when was about the last time

Mrs. Krumb called us up to try and get us to arrest her husband?"

It was one of them cases, sadly. Much as Krumb walked to work and therefore did not get fired from the museum earlier thanks to his crazy vehicle, Krumb's wife didn't draw attention to her black eyes and broken teeth only because she never left the house except to go to the liquor store, where nobody asked anybody else a question. Every time the cops dispatched to the Krumb residence, Mrs. would chicken out and decide she didn't want him arrested after all. The boys on call would offer to separate 'em, and Krumb would voluntarily go sleep in the science museum for the night.

Same thing every time their arguments reached a peak after a build-up of three or four months.

But never six, which is what it had been already.

"Wonder if anybody's seen her around," Hayward said when the lieutenant delivered the answer. "If we go over there and it's empty I might send you out to ask the neighbors...let's just see if we can get inside first, though. I got a bad feelin' about this."

Unfortunately, Sherriff Hayward was a man whose bad feelings were usually right.

Nobody answered the door when they knocked with the warrant, which was not unusual but also not ideal. Neither was the presence of Krumb's car alongside overgrown hedges necessarily meaningful, because, as previously stated, the man was known for walking to work or even long distances to save his money from going into his old truck's gas tank.

But when, on an impulse, Hayward tried the knob to find it unlocked, the Sheriff glanced over at his colleague.

With a quiet flick of the eyes down at the lieutenant's holster, Hayward rested a causal hand on his own and let himself into the house with a bellow.

"Claude? It's Sheriff Hayward! Your door's unlocked—the warrant says we gotta come in. Judge's orders."

The house was silent. Hayward braced himself for an angry old man to come stumbling down the stairs with a shake of his bony fist, but there was nothing like that.

Not even an old woman comin' to check on the ruckus.

Gesturing that his colleague should draw his gun, Hayward then nodded to the parlor and the rest of the house on the other side of the foyer.

His own sights set on the stairs, Hayward drew his own weapon and made his slow way to the second floor. Water ran.

You're never really prepared to see death, you know. No matter how many times you see it, it never gets easier. Hayward imagined that working in, say, the funeral industry might make it gentler, but as the sheriff of a small and mostly quiet town, Hayward was not strongly accustomed to finding dead bodies.

But, even with that being said—as dead bodies went, the murder-suicide of Mr. and Mrs. Krumb was one of the worst things the sheriff had ever seen with his own two eyes.

Something truly horrible had happened in this room, or maybe two horrible somethings. One corpse was desiccated, withered by time and a series of chemicals that could have ranged from lye to bleach to any damn thing else. Whatever the process was, it had gotten the old lady's body so it didn't stink as much as the old man's.

Probably, Krumb had shit himself. That was the coroner's problem, but it made Hayward gag so sharply that he had to cover his mouth and nose with his elbow or puke in the sink and spoil the crime scene. Bad enough to have all these chunks of flesh fused along the lower part of the wall and across the floor where Krumb, who must have been rolling around in agony, lay face-down in his own blood, his face mutilated and one exposed eye socket staring incredulously into the floor.

But that smell really put it over the top.

"Never mind," said Hayward, gagging into his elbow even as he slammed the bathroom door shut. "I found 'em...both of 'em."

"Dead?"

"You check on 'em and tell me...you know what?"

Feeling a little green, definitely in need of fresh air, Hayward made his way down the stairs and removed his hat to fan himself.

"I think I'm gonna let *you* call this one in, lieutenant...I'll get some fresh air and follow up with the neighbors myself."

Even once he was outside, the smell of dead old man shit burned the hair off the sheriff's nostrils. He felt so sick he politely refused cookies from Nancy Leiter, which was normally a difficult thing to do—but, after seeing all that, there were some questions to answer.

Based on the comments of the folks who answered their door, Mrs. Krumb used to at least take a neighborhood constitutional about two or three times a week: walking around the block in the early hours, or sometimes at night. Of the five people he asked while investigators, coroners, and even a journalist gathered at the crime scene, two witnesses had belatedly noted Mrs. Krumb wasn't taking her walks about two weeks prior, but, not knowing her, didn't stop to wonder; one had vaguely known her, but hadn't noticed she was missing her walks; the other two had noticed quickly and assumed she had died.

Sometimes it was just so damn dissatisfying to be right.

Finally, seeing the boys were dragging ass on getting the crime scene wrapped up, Hayward decided to hold off on going back into the building. Instead, he radioed in the information that it had been many weeks since the old lady's last appearance.

"Think I'm gonna walk on down to the museum where he used to work and ask the folks there if they saw any change in him, and when. Over."

"Roger that, over."

Humming, fixing the hat atop his head again, Sheriff Hayward made his way down the Smokeland sidewalks and toward the science museum that was a little under a mile away.

Ah, Smokeland! He loved it. Sure, a little aptly smoky during the summertime due to all the wildfires, but it was a damn cute town and the people in it were good as gold. It was the kind of place where a man could spend the rest of his life.

A place too good for the sorry sight Hayward had just seen.

Why'd the old man do it? Would there be a note somewheres? Must have been guilt over his wife, finally catalyzed by losin' his job...but damn. That was one brutal death scene; one awful way to die. Hopefully that journalist would keep things classy. Hayward didn't like the thought of folks gettin' upset.

Was *he* upset?

Maybe a little, but ultimately there was nothin' he could have done to stop Krumb. He had no way of knowing the old man was suicidal.

Whenever somebody died, though, there was always the 'if only.' If only Hayward had found probable cause to arrest him at the time of the initial voluntary interview. If only the judge had spent a little less time talkin' and a little more time signin'.

If only Hayward had listened to the witness and gotten the warrant for Roger Garnet and the science museum.

Buses sat on the far side of the museum's parking lot, their idle drivers napping or reading but otherwise forced to spend most of the day stuck in their vehicles; presumably so kids could eat lunch on the bus, or somesuch. Hayward squinted, pausing to read the names of the school districts plastered upon them. He whistled. Griffon? Some drive! He never knew their science museum had such pull—always seemed to him like such a small, rinky-dink operation that it was impressive anybody'd drive all that way to see it.

Feeling pleased as he cut across the parking lot, Hayward decided he'd make sure to praise the maligned director.

And his foot had just hit the curb when screaming started on the heel of a nasty-sounding bang.

"Shooter!"

You didn't need to tell Sheriff Hayward that. He knew a gunshot when he heard one—but even if he hadn't heard the gunshot and the scream, he certainly would have been tipped off by the river of frightened children abruptly rushing from the school.

"Get low," he shouted, drawing his gun and hurrying against the stream of knee-high bodies, "get low, get away from the museum!"

The doors flew open to emit a new wave of escaping children. Through them, Hayward glimpsed a person with a red or possibly bloodstained shirt lying face-down in a pool of blood.

Cursing, Hayward remained by the doors to shepherd out fleeing students.

With one hand, he turned his radio on.

"Lieutenant, I'm gonna need back-up at the museum."

Gritting his teeth to see people in the lobby fleeing anywhere but through the entrance, the crisscross of bodies almost too much to follow even as adults inside contrived to control the flow, Hayward stepped back from the doors.

"And try not to take too long."

12

IF YOU ASKED Miranda, things took a turn for the annoying when Stacy walked in on them and their fascinating discovery; but when an unrelated incident inspired someone to scream that a shooter was in the museum, the girl had to close her eyes and take a deep breath.

"Come on," she whispered to Luther as the chaos unfolded around them, tugging him into the shadow room. Their goal, the basement, was so close—but they couldn't be seen with a duffel bag of guns when somebody dropped dead and somebody else had just screamed the "S-word."

"What just *happened*," whispered Luther, clearly frantic as they plunged into the darkness of the exhibit.

The shadow room was not the best place for them, but it was a better place to hide than anywhere out on the main floor. The adults remaining had to be out of the way before the kids made a break for the basement. If not, Luther and Miranda risked being waylaid and, in the process of being turned back to the front doors, discovered.

Nothing could ever be easy, though. Paine loomed into the shadow room with them, the big wolf's frame illuminated by the light that flashed every forty seconds to capture the shadows of museum-goers upon colorful light-sensitive walls. As they hurried around the corner to the back of the exhibit and the red wall where a few kids trembled, the wolf lumbered with them.

"Get out of here," she urged them, "go to the front doors! Go on, they're evacuating."

Roused to action by her words, the smaller children rushed out. With a sigh of relief to find themselves alone, Miranda set the bag of guns down on the floor and let the boys have the argument she could sense brewing from the wolf's first howl of laughter.

"I can't believe that even worked! I was expected the works to clog up, or something—"

Luther glanced sharply at him. "What do you mean?"

"The golf ball! In the—the pressure thingie out there. Phew! Hilarious. I mean, I thought it would cause a problem, not absolute chaos."

"*You* did that?"

Grabbing the wolf by the front of his fur coat and staring up at him in shock, the boy asked with a tone of desperation, "Why? Why would you do that, Paine?"

Paine shrugged, spreading his paws. "Just thought it'd be good for a laugh. Why do I do anything?"

"You should thank him," said Miranda, checking the clip of the rifle in her hands before passing it to Luther and taking the next one. Luther took it automatically, his mind elsewhere.

"*Thank* him! For killing somebody? For getting us into this mess?"

"It takes one mess to cover another," responded the girl, checking her gun as she had checked the first before rising to her feet. "We have to move quickly, so let's leave this behind for now."

"What are we doing?"

"If we move fast, we can kill the witnesses who can tie us to this incident, destroy the footage for the security cameras, and be out of here with the rest of the evacuees before the building is even surrounded by SWAT officers."

"SWAT officers! Oh, man."

The boy's lamentation turned into a yelp as Miranda sent a hail of bullets into the floor. Wincing at the peal of gunfire, Luther demanded, "What are you doing?"

"Getting people to evacuate faster. Try to relax, Luther."

One hand landing earnestly on his shoulder amid a bright flash that froze their conjoined shadows to the wall, Miranda promised him, "Everything will work out, as long as you keep trying."

"But people are dying—going to die," said Luther miserably. "I don't think I can kill anybody. At least, I hope I can't."

She sighed. "Then *I'll* kill the witnesses. It doesn't matter. Either way, they have to die before the information gets out."

"Good idea," agreed Paine, following them as they made for the exit door.

Luther stopped, his teeth gritting as he whipped his head toward Paine.

"'Good idea,'" mocked the boy. "Where are you going this time? Going to go sabotage something else?"

Paine balked, his muzzle opening in shock while one great paw rested upon his fuzzy chest. "What's that supposed to mean?"

The words burst out of Luther with such outrage that Miranda had to wonder how deep-rooted these problems with their friendship really were.

"It's supposed to mean, "You killed someone,"" the boy launched in, barely containing his volume. "You're always messing things up and blaming me for it. Miranda thinks I should thank you for causing a big mess, but really I should thank *her!* If she weren't here, if we weren't involved in—whatever this is, you probably would have ended up killing someone anyway, and she might not have been around to keep me from going down for you."

Th wolf's ears drooped as the boy went on.

"You always blame me, Paine. When the going gets rough, you're never there. You turn into a stuffed animal. Well— I need friends who are going to help me."

The boy swallowed hard, his eyes lowering to hear himself argue with his friend.

Briefly baring his fangs, Paine said with a wave at Miranda, "Oh, yeah? And I suppose she helped you by getting you into this mess with her invitation to break into the janitor's office with her?"

Luther said nothing, staring numbly down at the gun in his hands. Outside, the chaos had abated somewhat. Two people ran across the echoing lobby and out the front doors.

Paine looked between the two of them.

"I get it," said the wolf to himself, his tail also drooping now. Nodding, he said, "Yeah, I understand. I don't mean to get in the way."

Luther winced, looking up at his friend.

"It's not that!"

"No, no." With a wave of his paw, the wolf shook his muzzle and said, "No, you're right. I'm sorry, Luther, you're right. All I do is cause problems for you these days! You can't even trust me home alone for the length of a school day."

Though Luther looked relieved to hear this second of self-insight, that feeling was clearly short-lived. With a tap of his chin, Paine mimed a human in thought before, raising a digit of his paw, he enthused, "That's it, I know!"

Luther looked grimly up at him. "Know what?"

With a chuckle that sounded evil even to Miranda, the wolf rubbed his paws together and receded back into the shadow room as he spoke.

"What were you just saying to me, Luther? I don't want you to think I'm more trouble than I'm worth— that I'm destructive to you. I want to be of good use; want to help. So, I'm going to go help you now."

The boy looked like he was going to throw up again. "Help me with what?"

No response came.

"Paine?"

Still no response.

Luthor hurried back into the darkness and around the corner, to where they'd left the guns. Miranda only followed him to confirm the wolf was nowhere to be seen against the faintly glowing neon backdrop of light-sensitive paints.

"We should go to the basement now," she urged him, pulling his elbow amid another flash. "It's clear. If we move quickly—"

Luther made a choking noise that caused her to stop.

He was all right—just crying, looked like.

"Come on. What's the matter?"

Luther almost laughed through his tears at the question. "It's too much," said the boy miserably. "How can this possibly work out?"

"It can't with that attitude."

"But my friend—"

"He'll be back. Don't you think Paine loves you if he's causing chaos all around but never hurting you?" She paused. "*Does* he hurt you?"

"No," answered Luther miserably, wiping his nose on his windbreaker and then, realizing with wide eyes it was spattered with Stacy's blood, using his shirt to clean himself of snot and tears and the blood of another human being. "No, he doesn't hurt me. He's just a wolf. He just has instincts."

There was a difference between animal instinct and the alien inclinations of a being capable of teleportation, of appearing simultaneously (or variably) as a stuffed animal or wolf, and of causing wanton destruction by sabotaging machinery that was inaccessible to most adults, let alone most wolves.

"It's no wonder you're so patient with *me*," observed Miranda, leading Luther down to the nearby basement door. The empty lobby echoed eerily around them, the distant cries of kids holed up in the auditorium or far exhibit halls the only backdrop to their journey. She went on, her tone soft as a breath. "Well, I'm sure we'll be friends for a long time, so hopefully it will all be worth the trouble."

"I just want to get out of here. How are we going to find a way through this, really?"

Miranda shrugged as they made their way down the stairs. The basement hallway was pleasantly empty; save, of course for the music that grew louder as they approached the director's office.

"Like I said. As long as the witnesses are eliminated, who's to say what happened? It's easier to believe an adult did this than a couple of kids."

The gun at the ready, Miranda nodded that he should do the same.

"Let's make this quick," she said.

Though he looked reluctant, Luther nodded.

Miranda unlocked the door to the director's office and swept in, the muzzle of the gun whipping toward the corner.

Her breath hitched while, behind her, Luther charged in and looked like he had no idea where to point his rifle. She discovered this when she turned to exchange a grim look with her new friend.

"Notice anything missing?"

The closet door had been broken down; the chair had been upended.

Mr. Garnet and Mrs. Carraway were nowhere to be found.

Luther didn't even have time to gasp before the new spate of gunfire echoed from the second floor.

"I know it feels like you're in over your head," Miranda said, looking up at the ceiling and briskly back down at her friend.

While Luther's eyes, ringed with terror, fixed upon hers, she told him on no uncertain terms, "You just have to keep trusting me."

The look on his face said he didn't want to anymore, but didn't have a choice. Miserable, Luther contemplated the room for only another few seconds.

"So what do we do now?"

"The only thing we can do...one thing at a time."

13

DEBORAH CARRAWAY HAD known that Even girl was fucked up from the moment they set eyes on each other.

Oh, sure. It was easy to blame the parents, or find some other touchy-feely philosophical excuse that made room for the possibility other people were not malignant but simply misguided. These were the sorts of principles Mrs. Carraway espoused in daily conversation and in the teaching of schoolchildren.

But the inside of her head was the one place where she could have any opinion she wanted. And, in her opinion, some people were naturally unpleasant, the way some people were tall or short or athletic or gay. Some things were just decided in the womb, and some things went way beyond any of that.

That was the case with Miranda. Deb had *met* the Evens, and none of them made her feel as creepy as the girl who was, strictly speaking, the brightest in her class.

Part of the problem was that Miranda Even was incredibly snotty. Mrs. Carraway had plenty of flaws of her own, as her mother-in-law liked to remind her; but so far as she could tell, parents of this era were not particularly interested in teaching their kids how to address other adults. The same was true of the Evens, whose daughter made all number of witheringly rude comments that went without any sign of correction.

That little barb—did she think she was smarter than Miranda Even? A child?

The question blistered her...mostly because she knew she wasn't.

But that was the problem when it came to dealing with Miranda Even. Miranda clearly had an adult's intellect, and an adult's exceptionally morbid persuasion and outlook. Though she was only seven years old, she wasn't like a seven-year-old in anything but her appearance and total lack of social filter. This fact made Mrs. Carraway file the girl into some subconscious 'adult' category, which made the teacher think the resentful kinds of things she otherwise would have only felt for one of her fellow students at college.

Had the Even girl done anything more in her class than be a little rude? Well, no, not really. Miranda's other teachers from prior years—at least, the ones who hadn't prematurely retired and fled the country—tended to share the opinion that Miranda should be strongly discouraged from playing with her peers if at all possible, and should be permitted to read whatever book she wanted whenever she wanted, even in the middle of a lecture, simply to avoid the horrific consequences of her boredom.

So, Mrs. Carraway had done that. As a result, things with Miranda had gone relatively well. But there was still a mutual animosity: one fueled by Miranda's superior intellect. The girl knew she was smarter than her teacher and did not belong in the school, and the teacher knew she had nothing to teach this particular student. This therefore made Mrs. Carraway feel inferior, and made her question the quality of her career choice.

She had made a lot of questionable choices in life, Mrs. Carraway. Marrying Walter had been a very questionable choice. Got more questionable all the time. Maybe it was just turning thirty and some esoteric, hormonal change to her sense of smell, but she just swore her husband smelled like *ham* these days. Maybe he was jerking off more because she wasn't fucking him, so she smelled the sweat. That was probably what it was.

She just didn't *like* Walter. Frankly, she never really did, but Smokeland was an expensive town, and the idea of living in the neglected neighboring towns had kept her up at night her whole senior year of high school. Therefore, like so many girls living in America's small towns, rich or poor, Mrs. Carraway got hitched right after graduation and spent the next ten years of her life plunging into increasingly deep regret. Her own bratty kids were almost old enough to be in her class, and that mere thought had been enough to drive her into the arms of Roger Garnet.

Roger was sometimes a little annoying, but he was a funny sort of guy who screwed like a champ. Anything was better than Walter, who just laid there and received her effort. Roger actually seemed like a unicorn: a man who perceived sex as an actual two-way *interaction*.

And he was also, apparently, doing mushrooms behind her back.

Deborah fumed in the closet when those spooky little brats left, trying about ten minutes of screaming before, as "La Bamba" began, she gave up and leaned her forehead against the slats of the closet.

How the hell was she going to get out of this closet? Somebody was bound to free them eventually, but this was just humiliating. Locked up by a couple of kids!

And how had they gotten that door to slam shut so hard, anyway? It seemed amazing that a grown woman couldn't shove open a door against the strength of two children, let alone *one*. Deborah needed to work out, clearly.

"Roger! Roger, wake up!"

Still totally unconscious. That was just embarrassing...what the hell was his problem? She'd never seen anyone faint before, let alone a man—let alone, a man discovering children in his closet. You would have thought he found a serial killer waiting there. A ghost. a demon. Anything!

Well, that just went to show you that Deborah had to learn to pick her lovers a little better.

After trying to pound the door down to no avail, Mrs. Carraway studied the contents of the dingy closet and struggled to find anything that could be of help to her. So far as she could tell there were no lockpicks, no blowtorches, certainly nothing of any *dramatic* use. There were only the bobby pins in her hair, and she had absolutely no idea how to use those to open any kind of locked door.

There just weren't many options here.

Gritting her teeth, Mrs. Carraway looked around the closet and pulled down a thin lab coat whose sleeve she tore free. Wrapping this strip around her fist and taking a deep breath, Deborah focused on the slats before her.

She didn't know a lot about throwing punches, but Deb had the feeling it wasn't supposed to hurt quite so much. Her stomach lurched even with the protective covering of the cloth, the tilted slats of thin wood in the locked door sharp on contact with her fist.

Hissing, Mrs. Carraway hauled back and punched again. Her knuckles throbbed and she reeled against the pain, holding her sore fingers with one hand.

But one of the boards had snapped beneath her knuckle, and the hope let in just that much more light.

"Okay," whispered Mrs. Carraway to herself,

shaking off her fist before drawing back for the next punch, and the next.

Slowly, one slat at a time, the horizontal pieces of wood cracked beneath her fist. Each snapping piece bore its own price—another sharp sting across her knuckles—but the rush of dopamine that came to her at each success was like nothing she had ever experienced. Mrs. Carraway had not known herself to be claustrophobic, but in the given circumstances, the promise of freedom made her feel like a prisoner fresh from solitary confinement.

At last, with a cry of satisfaction and a victorious hefting high of a splintered fist that soaked blood through the lab coat fabric, Mrs. Carraway punched out enough boards to reach her hand through and grope for the locked handle. After sharply jerking it to find it immovable, the teacher's laugh of victory turned to a frustrated sob.

So she really was going to have to do this the hard way.

Upon smashing down a few more slats, first with her fist and then with the hard sole of one of her flats, Deborah studied the hole and cleaned its edges from as many obviously jagged chunks of wood as she could find.

There were still plenty, however. As, with a deep breath, Deborah struggled to contort her upper half through the new opening, a particularly sharp dart of wood jammed into her waist. The tearing of her flesh happened slowly enough for her to feel everything, and her profanity was stiff competition for those Mariachis.

"Deborah?"

Roger's voice, groggy from his deep unconsciousness and whatever fucking mushrooms he had eaten that morning, really pissed Deborah off.

"*Now* you're awake," she told him, halfway impaled on the broken slats of the closet door. "Some prince charming you are."

"What's going on?" The director had managed to work the necktie in his mouth down to his neck, probably while Deb was pounding out the slats of the closet door. Deborah focused on wiggling out of her prison, telling herself there would be time for all this later. She had already been stuck there for half an hour, maybe more, and would be damned if she spent even another minute there now that she had a way out.

Even if the splinters scratched long, deep cuts in her waist. She bit back her pain the way she bit back her untimely annoyance at the way Roger cried out for no reason.

"Where is it?"

"'It?' You mean, the kids?"

"What kids? You mean—" He whipped his head toward her, his eyes wide with shock. "You didn't see that wolf?"

Oh, God.

What a useless man Garnet was turning out to be.

Extricating herself fully from the closet and knocking a lot of nonsense off the top of the desk to do so, Deborah scowled down at the slits in her dress and the burning cuts that were beginning to become very noticeable beneath. Some areas were even staining with blood...how annoying. She'd ruined new clothes before, but this was ridiculous.

"Did you hear me?"

"I heard you," Deborah answered, dusting off her hands and sliding off the desk, "I don't even want to talk about it. You need serious help."

"Help? What are you talking about! Of course I need *help.* We *all* do! There's a giant wolf loose in this museum!"

Her hands pressing against her face, Deborah shut her eyes and told Roger, "There's no *wolf,* Roger. You're on psychedelic mushrooms you've been growing in the closet of your office."

"They don't give you *that* kind of hallucination," he told her tersely, rolling his eyes. "They don't give you 3D hallucinations at all, really—not when you microdose, definitely."

"'Microdose.' I should leave you tied up to this chair."

All the same, Deborah looked around for scissors with which to saw open the duct tape. Roger went on insisting, "I know what I saw. It was enormous! Tall as me, no—taller!"

God help her! Deborah's head throbbed with the stress. Her instinct was to say Roger needed a therapist, but Deborah needed a therapist of her own if she was ever going to figure out how to pick better men.

"How about you just shut up." she told him calmly, jamming the scissors down the duct tape at his wrists and passive aggressively poking him with the blunt instruments more than once in the process.

Screaming intense enough to pierce the mariachi music rocked them from above. Roger and Deborah looked sharply toward the ceiling, then at one another.

"If my principal doesn't expel that little psycho after today," Mrs. Carraway told her boyfriend, "I'm going to quit my job and set the school on fire, myself."

Roger shook his head, insisting, "Your nemesis, the Even girl? Nah. All that screaming, they probably saw that wolf up there—don't look at me like that! I can't believe you didn't see it."

Shaking her head with serious displeasure, Deborah assured him, "I didn't see anything, and whatever is going on upstairs has nothing to do with any wolf."

"Damn it, Deborah! As long as you've known me, haven't I been honest with you?" At her sustained look of displeasure before cutting his torso free of the chair, Roger spread his hands and added, "About *most* things?"

"You disgust me, Roger."

"Deborah!"

His total inability to take responsibility for his lies or his apparent psychotic break irked Deborah so much that she dropped the scissors on the floor and told him, "Let yourself out. I'm going to go find someone sane to help me deal with this."

"Deborah, please—"

Ignoring his begging, Deborah Carraway strode into the hall. Her steps were wincing in an effort to keep her side from bleeding too much, but there was really no stopping the marks from weeping a little with every jostle. Almost numb with the strange, insane doings, Deborah did not even try to begin sorting out the events of the last hour. Her only priority was to get a few more adults involved in wrangling the Even girl and her little 'boyfriend,' and then making sure they were never a part of any civilized society ever again.

Of course, when Deborah emerged from the basement, there were no adults to be seen. Only a few students still scrambling for the front, rear, and side doors, screaming every now and again in the echoing exhibit hall.

And the dead intern, face-down in a pool of blood with a golf ball-sized hole in the back of their cranium.

Deborah's limbs tingled with an electric shock of fear that told her to run.

And she wanted to run for the front doors, but when the Even girl emerged from the shadow room with an AR-15 in one hand the strange boy's elbow in the other, Deborah did the only thing that seemed like it might protect her.

She ducked into the Hall of Optical Illusions.

Much like the shadow room, the Hall of Optical Illusions was constructed in an almost mazelike structure. It was styled after a fun fair house of horrors, with a circus theme pervading everything from the font chosen on the signs to the frames in which the two-dimensional optical illusions were prominently displayed.

To Deborah's surprise, the hall seemed empty. She had expected to find a cluster of students or even chaperones holed up within, but she was greeted by only a big-nosed witch who looked back on dreams of her beautiful youth.

That hopefully meant that the chaperones had done a good job of getting the students out...which meant Deborah wasn't going to worry about them.

Some people were heroic in the face of disaster. Deborah, like many teachers anxiously aware of the distant but grim possibility, pored over the headlines in the days after school shootings, reading and re-reading anecdotes of heroic survivors who disarmed gunmen (or gunchildren, in most cases) while exposing themselves to incredible bodily harm.

Those people were fascinating and very impressive, but Deborah just wasn't that sort of person. She was barely a teacher; certainly not a hero. She couldn't teach any kids at all ever again if she were killed in a shooting.

So, she was just going to have to sequester herself here for a few minutes and hope the coast would clear. As long as the kids went literally anywhere else, she would just have to run to the front door of the museum. Then, she'd be home free.

Meanwhile, was there a back door to this place?

While Deborah wandered, passing impossible cubes and endless stairs, a peal of gunfire rattled in the lobby. Gritting her teeth, Deborah hurried her pace into the depths of the maze and turned a corner that seemed like it had ought to be the last.

And she did find an emergency exit door...along with, of all things, a small stuffed wolf.

Deborah would have laughed if she were in better humor—if anything made any sense. In the midst of the bizarre nightmare of gunfire and the unceasing pressure on her brain to escape with her life, Deborah could not truly place or appreciate the significance of the little toy in the dead center of the floor. She glanced at it, her brain searching for the conversation that gunfire had driven out of her head, and came up with nothing.

Without its significance, Deborah wrote the wolf off.

Deborah rushed on to the door labeled EXIT, which opened to a dimly lit back hallway intended for staff.

Once again, an EXIT sign confronted her; this,

glowing at the end of the hall with a little arrow in an indication that she could follow the corner to a quick way out.

Her muscles beginning to relax with a crisis averted, Deborah made her ginger way toward it.

Something growled behind her.

Deborah stopped a few steps into her journey

"Roger?"

As Deborah turned around, the dim lights snapped off.

Darkness draped the corridor.

"This isn't funny," she said sharply. "We don't have time for this."

The growling continued, low and vicious.

Deborah stumbled back a step, her palms sweating.

"Something serious is going on. A shooting. This is no time for a prank. I told you. I don't care about your—"

Something tall and fast rushed at her in the dark.

Deborah screamed and turned to run, sprinting for the red words pointing her way to freedom.

The wolf snatched her up by a thick fistful of her flowing red locks before she'd even reached the corner.

Howling as her screaming increased—as Mrs. Carraway reached up to scratch at the paw that held her—the towering monster bared its fangs and snarled in her face. Deb screamed, tears rolling down her cheeks, her body overcome by fear greater than any she had ever felt in her life.

The hot terror dripped down Mrs. Carraway's legs. Roger had been right.

With one great paw still holding onto her hair, the wolf tore away the fabric of her dress.

Deborah screamed. She slapped at the beast's muzzle only to nearly vomit with pain when its jaws snapped upon her hand. The bear-trap force was more than sufficient to break an animal's neck: her hand stood no chance.

While her bones snapped, Deborah sobbed to be splattered in the face by her own blood. The drooling monster tore its bloody fangs from her hand and pushed her arm away, freeing her exposed neck.

Now it repeated the hard mechanical action of its snapping jaw, this time severing Mrs. Carraway's vocal cords and breaking her spine all in the same bite.

Mercifully, Mrs. Carraway lost most of her feeling after that.

Horribly, Mrs. Carraway did not die.

Now that her body was limp, the wolf dropped her to the floor like a ragdoll. She did still feel her head slam into the concrete, though it blurred her vision in an intense explosion of pain. Even if she felt it, however, she wouldn't have been able scream about it, owing to the bite that pulsed more blood from her neck every time her heart beat.

Stooping over the bleeding woman, the wolf gave her stomach one long, thoughtful lick before peeling its lips back from its fangs.

Without delay, it sank its jaws into her flesh.

While the wolf tore off a great mouthful of skin and muscle, Mrs. Carraway marveled.

She'd always expected her intestines to be pinker than that, somehow.

14

LUTHER WAS BEGINNING to worry that Miranda had over-estimated her ability to stay out of real trouble.

How could she be so certain that was her "thing," anyway? It was defined by a negative. You could only "prove" you had this "thing" as long as the undesirable event didn't happen to you. Heck! You could say that you were immortal, and could plausibly be so until the day you got hit by that train.

So, as Luther and Miranda stood on the edge of the empty basement office, Luther had to wonder if Miranda had not perhaps put a little too much stock in a streak of good fortune.

And if that were the case, he was really screwed.

Looked like he was just going to have to believe in Miranda until further notice—until he found his own way out of this situation, or Paine did.

Paine!

While sorrow washed over the boy to think of his friend, Miranda pushed him back into the hall and observed of the gunfire from the floor above, "Either the SWAT is already in here, or someone found the guns. Either way, we should go figure out what we're dealing with."

Luther nodded lamely, the new chaos having faded into the background of his consciousness beneath the discovery of the missing teachers. He wanted to ask her how they were going to solve that problem, but, well...Miranda was right.

Whether by the SWAT or by Brock and his gang, getting cornered in the basement would be seriously bad news.

Thankfully, the gunfire was the (ir)responsibility of the latter.

While Luther and Miranda crouched by the door at the top of the concrete stairwell, another few rounds were fired off amid boyish laughter. "This really is harder than it looks in games. There's so much— what do you call it."

"Recoil," Dingus answered, "can I try?"

"That's it! Recoil. Hey, Dingus, go set up some of the jars from the gift shop over there, put 'em in those windows."

Beneath Miranda's gentle hand, the door to the lobby cracked open in time to catch sight of Dingus darting beneath Brock's instruction. Based on Dingus's trajectory, Brock and his crew seemed to be at such an angle that the door, when opened, would block them from view—maybe even give Brock an advantage if he had as flighty a trigger finger as Miranda.

Stacy's death replayed in Luther's mind, but he tried to tell himself there was nothing that could be done now. And, anyway...he had seen worse.

The body itself wasn't what bothered Luther; nor was the loss of his frenemy. That, of course, was horrible, but the emotions there were factors still yet to be processed by his young mind amid so much other trauma.

What bothered Luther was that, in all other ways, Miranda was so controlled. So measured. She seemed to reason out the smallest decisions.

And she didn't flinch.

He wasn't really sure what he thought about Stacy's death.

"We'll have to move quickly," she whispered, stirring him from his thoughts and eliciting a nod. "Go on three. One—two—"

Dingus clunked down a jar of something heavy in the windowsill between the lobby and the gear workshop. As, announced by his squeaking sneakers, he sprinted off to get another target, Miranda sprang into motion with her gun at the ready.

Luther followed as fast as he could, then froze.

Beneath the slowly spinning rover, Brock and two of his three cronies stood with the remainder of the janitor's armaments.

"So it's *you two* responsible for this?"

Brock almost looked impressed, then pissed; then, he laughed. "I should have known," he said, looking over at his friends. "Total weirdos."

Luther tried to take another step out but Brock whipped the gun at him, his unpracticed aim still dangerous.

"I hope you realize how it would look if the police burst in right now," Miranda said, staring the stupider boys down.

"Looks to me like I could be a hero!" Brock's eyes sparkled, his smile growing genuine for a handful of seconds. "Hell yeah, I could—hell yeah. I found the gunman's guns and saved the day. Who'll argue with that?"

"Anybody who's ever talked to you for more than two or three seconds," Luther answered.

"It's our word against yours," agreed Miranda, her AR-15 far more expertly held as she aimed the gun for Brock's head. "I can take one look at you and know that adults discuss you as much as they discuss me… maybe more."

Brock bared his teeth. His arms tensed.

Would he really shoot? How could they hope to take out all three bullies before at least one of them managed a killing shot?

Somewhere in the museum, a woman's scream drew the attention of everyone but Miranda.

While the boys' heads jerked toward the peril, the girl whipped the sights of her rifle up to the rover and fired.

Dingus cried out, as did the member of gang who managed to slip away from the falling model. The one to the right screamed as he was pinned.

Brock had no time to scream, but the rover crushed his skull in just the right place to cause his finger to tighten.

The M16 unloaded its clip in a long, uncontrolled burst that sent bullets flying wildly across the lobby.

Miranda dragged Luther down to the floor. Glass shattered; marbles from the gift store went rolling through the lobby and across the gear workshop, amid the spark of electrical equipment and the rolling fog of a burst fire extinguisher.

Luther almost would have imagined himself happy that his bully was gone, or afraid to see the corpse, or something. Alarmingly, he felt nothing at all about it other than a vague sense of relief that he had yet to take a life.

After the corpse's finger went limp and the hail of automatic gunfire stopped, the horrified wailing of at least one of the remaining boys rose to a high crescendo. It was hard to tell if it was the one pinned under the rover with the corpse, or the one who still held his plundered pistol—albeit, with trembling hands.

"You killed him! Brock and I were supposed to get married someday!"

"So he really was gay," remarked Miranda with a hint of pride, scrambling up and retreating to the stairwell. "I knew it...Luther!"

The weeping toady had turned his pistol upon the exposed Watson boy. With a brisk glance around, Luther dashed to the front desk and managed to slide behind it without slipping on the marbles still rolling across the floor.

And, unfortunately, Dingus made it to the rover without incident.

Luther expected him to lift the great model to free his pinned friend. Instead, in typical sociopath bully style, Dingus took the M16 from his dead friend's hand and sneered at the pieces of brain matter that attached themselves to his fingers. Delaying to wipe this off on his shorts, he had just enough time to raise the rifle before Miranda popped around her cover and opened fire.

"Miranda!"

"No one can see us and live," she answered above the sound of her rapport.

Despite the girl's uncanny aim, the remaining toadies were small and quick. Seeing they took shelter behind the rover, Miranda laid off to assess risk and study the environment.

"I need you to cover me," she said to Luther.

His stomach clenched. "What? Why?"

Too late...Luther should have known there was no time for questions on the battlefield. Her rifle cradled to her breast, Miranda dashed into the open and made a break for the shadow room.

The bully with the pistol leapt into the open, firing wildly while weeping for his lost love.

"Watch out!"

Before Luther knew what had happened, his video game instincts took over. The rifle's sights trained themselves on the bully; his finger did the firing.

He watched a tile shatter at the bully's feet, then gasped with horror to watch his head explode all the same. While Dingus shouted from the other side of the rover, Luther whipped his head over in time to see Miranda lower her gun and duck into the shadow room.

As much as he wanted to, it wasn't safe to join her.

Screaming like an action star, Dingus did what he should have done two minutes prior and lifted the rover off his surviving friend.

While the boy wheezed, one arm across his broken ribs until he realized the nearness of the abandoned gun.

Luther barely had a chance to notice as Dingus dropped the rover and whipped his gun toward the desk.

At the new burst of fire, Luther dropped behind his cover with his hands over his ears. Tears filled his eyes.

This was insane! If he got out of this, he was going to have nightmares for the rest of his life. *More* nightmares, anyway. What the hell was he going to do? How was Paine going to protect Luther from his own guilt?

For that matter...where had Paine gone?

Luther's stomach twisted in terrible anxiety. Was the wolf coming back? Surely he was—he always did—but it would have been a real comfort to have his old friend by his side during these moments of duress. The wolf wasn't just a friend and a sometimes questionable influence, after all. He was also a guardian to Luther, who was an anxious boy in an anxiety-producing world.

At a break in the noise, Luther sprang up to return fire with the weapon braced against the desk. Bullets went flying, bouncing off the rover and knocking pieces off of it but otherwise proving ineffective.

Then, Luther's gun clicked empty.

Gasping in horror, the boy shook the weapon as though it were a malfunctioning watch. He pulled the trigger again.

Nothing.

On the other side of the rover, Dingus leapt up with the M16 at the ready.

While his face contorted into an expression of vile hatred for his friends' killer, Miranda sprinted out of the shadow room to launch something as though it were a shotput.

For a few seconds, Luther wasn't sure what it was that Miranda had launched. He hadn't seen the exact number of arms in the bag and certainly hadn't seen anything smaller than a rifle. Even the pistol wielded by the supine boy had been a bit of a surprise.

But, as the object arced to the other side of the rover, and Miranda sprinted back into the darkness of the shadow room, Luther's instincts told him to duck.

The reality of the grenade was settled with an explosion.

Screaming boys and blasting rubble drowned Luther's cry. He clapped his hands over his ringing ears and grimaced, the rifle falling to his knees. His eardrums felt like they were going to burst. The explosion took with it all sound except the long, shrill keen of nothingness.

Miranda had made it to his side and threw her hands upon his shoulders, shaking him from his stupor. Her mouth moved rapidly and he lowered his hands from his ears, trying to match her lips to the soft noises that gradually slipped in above and around the ringing.

"—We have to go," she was saying. "Now—there isn't much time."

Miranda pulled him to his feet and rushed him across the smoking lobby. With a cry for the charred bodies beneath the rubble of the rover model, Luther averted his eyes and focused on the destination.

"Roger Garnet," called a loudspeaker, a million

miles away so far as Luther's ears were concerned, "this is your chance to surrender! Come out with your hands up in thirty seconds or *we'll* come in. We have the place surrounded: you don't have a chance."

"We have to give up," hissed Luther miserably, even as Miranda hustled him past the cardboard cut-out before the locked door of the janitor's office.

"No, we don't. There's still four witnesses on the loose somewhere in this building. We have to do something about them and erase the security footage. That's all it will take to get us out of this, you understand? It's nothing."

With a brisk push, Miranda threw open the door and looked as close to frustrated as Luther had yet to see her.

Much like in the basement, the hostages were gone—but, with the door still locked and the panel in the ceiling in obvious disarray, at least it was obvious this time where they'd disappeared to.

"Looks like we have to split up," Miranda said with a grim flick of her eyes toward the ceiling. "Hold on, let me load your gun."

"What do you mean?"

With the weapon still around Luther's shoulders, Miranda drew a clip from the pocket of her dress and set about reloading for him. "I mean, I have to find a computer terminal—unless you know how to get into a locked administrative PC without knowing the password."

Misery wrapping around him like a dark cloak, the boy looked up at the ladder again and said, "But—I thought you said *you* were going to—to kill the teachers—"

"Survival of the fittest is a matter of adaptability to change, not of strength or intelligence. If you want to survive, Luther, you're going to have to adapt. And I believe that you can."

Though Miranda stepped back and seemed about to turn away, she paused and threw her arms around his neck.

Luther gasped as the uncanny girl hugged him, her embrace tight with the hope of another meeting and the fear that it might not happen.

He tried not to sob, but tears danced in his eyes all the same.

While Miranda released him, glass shattered in the lobby to permit the fast-tromping boots of what, for all it mattered to the young boy, could have been a hundred men.

Luther scrambled up the ladder and tried not to look back—or to look too far ahead.

15

FOR A MICRODOSE, Roger Garnet was sure on one bad trip.

Like all bad trips, he'd put himself on it. He'd gotten a bad girlfriend in a bad way; he'd been depressed while trying to skate by at a disorganized museum and had responded by growing mushrooms at said museum for his microdosing experiments, which he had felt at the time to provide some form of plausible deniability but which he now realized was a career-ruining mistake; and, of course, he had told his lame girlfriend about the giant wolf that was in the closet with those two creepy kids.

Roger really had to learn to think a thing through before he made a decision...even a simple one like opening his mouth was fraught with peril.

He just had to hope that Deborah could take care of herself.

Frankly, seeing that wolf, Roger wasn't so sure *he* was safe, either. That thing was massive, and, for the record, very real. Roger saw it with his own two eyes, represented in all three dimensions. It was a physical thing, not a trick of the light or some odd shadow in the depths of the closet.

Just thinking about it gave Roger the heebie-jeebies. He had to get out of here—had to call the cops.

Deborah had unbound his wrists, but the duct tape had been applied under his arms, around his ribs, and around his waist and hips. The kids had stuck him to the chair with prejudice and so, in spite of his best efforts to coordinate both his feet and his hands, Roger couldn't manage to get the scissors into his clutches.

Cringing, he readied himself for the landing and rocked back and forth in the chair.

Though he'd been braced, slamming his face into the cold concrete floor of the unfinished basement office was just not a good time.

The connection rang through his head like a wind chime, reverberating down his spine and to the very tips of his toes. While he winced, he groped around on the floor before him and got the scissors.

At least the next part was easy. After hacking away at the duct tape, Roger was up and ready to call the cops.

Well—almost ready to call the cops. He was about to find the phone cord when those two creepy kids came rushing down the hall and Roger had to vault the desk. While he hid under it, out of everyone's sight but the psychedelic mushrooms at the end of the closet, the situation went from bad to worse. Gunfire erupted upstairs.

Was Deborah okay? Who cared? Where the hell was that wolf?

What was he going to do with those mushrooms?

It was such a waste to destroy them...but he was going to have to do something.

Delaying only a few seconds after the coast was clear and the kids had gone to look elsewhere, Roger decided to eat the entirety of his crop.

The situation was already incredibly bad. It was possible he was going to die. If so, he wanted to die on psychedelic mushrooms. And if he didn't die, any odd behavior could be explained away as shock. A small price to pay in exchange for saving himself any number of felonies related to the growth and consumption of psychedelic mushrooms in an educational facility.

After cramming his mouth full of about sixteen mushrooms of various shapes and sizes and groaning in disgust at the almost burning taste of too much mushroom flesh, Roger forced his hyper-salivating mouth to masticate the fungi while he rushed around the office in search of the phone cord.

One was buried in the bottom of his desk drawer.

He had the landline plugged in and 911 dialed in seconds, though he had to strain to hear over the racket of gunfire upstairs.

"911, what's your—"

"I'm at the museum," cried Roger. "My name's Roger Garnet, I'm the director of the science museum! You need to send your guys in here to get me out."

The operator paused for a few long seconds. "Let me patch you through to the Sheriff, sir."

What the hell was this, the science museum's front desk? Roger thought you just called 911 and emergency crews were dispatched based on your needs—nobody ever said anything about repeating your story multiple times like you were trying to get a bill sorted out at the cable company.

After a few seconds of kitschy hold music, a man's gruff voice picked up.

"This is Sheriff Hayward."

"Sheriff," said Roger hurriedly, wrapping the cord around his hand in a custom retained since childhood, "it's Roger Garnet—you've got to come in and get me out, Hayward. I'm in the museum."

"We know you are," answered the sheriff coolly. "How about you just calm down and reason this out with me."

"You can't imagine what's going on in here! The kids are after me, and there's some kind of—"

He had started to say there was a wolf stalking the halls, but the idea seemed bad to share at this very moment. The sheriff cut him off, anyway.

"The kids aren't after you, Roger. How about you just put down your guns, and—"

"Guns? What—"

No way.

The director's jaw dropped, a last piece of hastily chewed mushroom falling from his lip.

Did they think *he* was the one doing all this?

"Now, hold on just a minute! These aren't *my* guns, Sheriff—"

"There's no use denyin' it, Garnet. Claude Krumb told us all about it before he shot himself. Surprised you didn't invite him to join you—or didn't you know about his dead wife in the bathtub at home?"

The color, whatever remained of it, drained from Roger's face. While the most intense exchange of gunfire yet rattled the floor above, Roger strained to turn down the mariachi music. The landline phone crept to the edge of the desk, the cord not quite long enough to stretch. While reaching, he protested, "I didn't know anything about a murder!"

"Who said anything about a *murder*, Roger? I just said she was dead."

"Give me a break. I'm going to be dead soon, too, if you don't come in here and do something!"

Suddenly the line was muffled, as though Sheriff Hayward had put a hand over the receiver. All the same, Roger made out the key element of his words.

"—think he's threatenin' to shoot himself."

Balking, Roger finally reached the radio and snapped it off while shouting, "No, I—"

The clatter of the phone as it fell to the floor ended the conversation with the hard disconnection of the line.

At the same time, an explosion rocked the museum.

Sick to his stomach with the mushrooms and the chaos, Roger dropped the phone and dashed out into the hall.

All right. He was going to have to go out, dodge the real shooter, and meet the cops—show them he was innocent and a victim in all of this, much as anyone else in the museum.

But maybe not quite as much as the kids.

On emerging from the basement, Roger gasped in sorrow. The scene was devastating on a personal level, for as deeply as he loved the museum—but adding in the dead bodies of the intern and the charred remains of what looked to be students made Roger's heart break in two.

Who were these? Were these the children who had locked him and Deborah in the office?

A door slammed somewhere while, outside, a megaphone warned Roger to surrender.

Kneeling, Roger pushed rover scraps off the bodies. After lifting one particularly long piece of rubble from the blast, he peered into their faces.

No—he didn't recognize these kids at all.

All these bodies, and neither the boy nor the girl were among them.

His brain crawled with panic. Because his reflex was to hug the ailing children before him, he instead hugged the piece of metal that he had pulled off of the central body.

The doors blew open and SWAT members surged into the museum.

With a womanly scream, Roger dashed around the administrative desk and into the gear workshop, broken glass crunching and marbles scattering with his stride.

"He's armed," bellowed one of the officers.

Roger glanced down at the piece of metal, still held in his arms only because of the mushrooms and the way the affected his consciousness.

With another little cry, he realized what it was and barely managed to avoid dropping the assault rifle in total shock.

A spray of bullets whizzed past his hip as he ran for his life. Roger screamed, ducking between puzzle stations and rushing toward a series of desks that, along with the wall adjacent, formed a hall to the staff section.

All he had to do was get there before somebody shot him.

"Drop your weapon and get down on the ground!"

The commands came every few steps amid a lot of gunfire and other forms of shouting this or that esoteric military command. Stopping to obey before he had cover would only get him killed.

Nearly skidding around the corner, Roger avoided the bees buzzing behind their glass, redirected to the door at the end of the hall, and sprinted to freedom.

He had just dropped a hand on the knob and found it happily unlocked when another voice barked behind him, "Freeze!"

He did, sighing deeply.

"Drop. Your. Weapon."

Roger glanced down at the burden in his hands, happy to comply if nobody would shoot him before he could.

Just as he leaned down to obey, one of the cops slipped on a marble in his rush to be the second at the scene of the arrest.

Crying aloud, this second officer slid forward and smashed head-first into the window of the bee exhibit.

The furious buzzing began at once, but it had grown into the thunderous accompaniment of a great black storm by the time the rest of the officers had Roger in their sights. The only competition for the all-encompassing drone was the screams of the officers as, seeking bare flesh, the bees swarmed the only features they could find on the SWAT officers: namely, their faces and wrists. As the screaming grew to a frenzy, more bees, attracted by the pheromones of their dying relatives, came sweeping into the fray.

When one zipped toward Roger, he realized it was time to go and threw open the door.

As officers retreated and some even wasted a few bullets firing wildly at the bees around, Roger stuck his foot right into Deborah Carraway's open torso.

Crying sharply, Roger sprang out of his former lover and only remembered to shut the door upon hearing a voice that sounded suspiciously like Sheriff Hayward as it shouted, "Where the fuck do you think you're goin'?"

Alone at last, Roger shook Deborah off his pant leg and tried not to puke.

Oh, Deborah! What had happened? Roger's eyes watered. He leaned down to touch her face, expecting to find it cold and still.

But it wasn't.

It was still warm.

Gasping in horror, Roger turned on the nearby light and peered through the dim at her still twitching face. The rapid convulsions of her muscles seemed linked to her broken spine, which was exposed in several places within the meat of her neck. While her eyelids and lips all fluttered without rhyme or reason, Roger made one morbid glance down at her torso and regretted it.

This was the wolf's doing. Roger was sure of it. Nothing else in this museum could have torn her apart like this— broken her spine like this. Not even an assault rifle.

With a miserable glance at his girlfriend and then at the gun in his hands, Roger pointed the slightly dented weapon at her forehead.

He pulled the trigger and hoped it still worked.

16

THE NEXT FOIBLE was Miranda's fault, really. She let her attention waver and, after the encounter with Brock, her confidence was getting the better of her.

The line between faith and hubris was a fine one, and sometimes Miranda was in the habit of overstepping.

While Luther hustled up the ladder and wiggled into the ceiling after his own teachers, Miranda shifted the gun around to her back and crouched by the janitorial office's door.

Out in the lobby of the museum—and the gear workshop, judging by the sound of an angry swarm that soon joined all the banging, barking, firing, and rushing—the SWAT searched the museum for the shooter.

Interestingly enough, however, they seemed to be confused as to just who that shooter was.

The patsy had presented himself. Assuming this would end the way these things frequently did—suicide by cop—all Miranda had to do was make sure Luther completed his side of the job while she cleared the footage and confirmed Mrs. Carraway.

A wholly utilitarian kill, of course.

No personal pleasure in it at all.

When the SWAT started screaming and the furious buzzing rose to a terrible crescendo, Miranda slipped out of the janitor's office and leaned around the cardboard cut-out.

"Where the fuck do you think you're goin'?"

The sheriff was the least armored man there, yet the only one who remained unflinching in the face of the bees. While thrashing cops shrieked and misfired their guns—sometimes throwing the weapons down altogether to flee the museum—Miranda took advantage of the Sheriff's inattention.

Head low, steps fast, Miranda swept through the museum's main floor. Across the wide lobby, around the crater from the grenade and all the rover (and human) pieces, down beneath the other side of the administrative desk.

Once there, Miranda emitted a tiny sigh of exasperation.

The firefight with Luther's bullies had left the PC of the entrance a smoking, sometimes sparking pile of glass and metal casing.

Thinking fast, Miranda considered Roger's PC and nodded to herself.

The path down to the basement was easy by now. After she ducked out from the desk to find Sheriff Hayward had disappeared for the moment, the girl hurried along the wall to the basement door and sprinted down its stairs to reach the director's office.

Miranda's first mistake was leaving the door unlocked. She was confident not only that she could be fast, but that she would hear anyone coming down the hall or the stairs—certainly any noisy SWAT officer.

The PC on the desk had been unplugged to accommodate the furniture being moved around. She therefore engaged in her second mistake—slipping off the AR-15 and leaning it against the desk so she could slide underneath and get the bundle of tangled cords still stuck to their foot-long power strip—without even thinking. Preoccupied as she was, Miranda had not considered it a motion unto itself, so much as part of a greater, incomplete action.

The third mistake was giving into the temptation presented by Dan's mushroom tank.

After all—the tank meant that there had to be a plug somewhere in the closet. How else was the light functioning? Finding and using it seemed like it would save Miranda time over trying to move the entire desk and all the things upon it, especially by herself. So, after grabbing the bundle of cords, Miranda fed them up through the hole in the desk and clambered atop it to pull them to the closet side of the impromptu barrier.

The click of the gun had her dropping the cords and whipping around to catch the thief, but too late.

"Don't even try it!"

Of course.

Miranda had accounted for SWAT officers and tricky teachers—but the girl who took for granted the fact that she was smarter than her peers never even thought for a second that someone her own age could sneak up on her.

"Put your hands up."

Miranda raised her hands, studying the girls standing on the floor beneath her with the vague sense of recognition shown for the faces of a dream upon waking.

"I know you two," she said at last. "You're Stacy's friends."

"Did you kill her?"

"So you found the body." She paid special attention to the armed girl who was asking most of the questions. The gun was amateurishly held and easily disarmed if Miranda could just get a chance to grab it. "Shouldn't you both have evacuated with the rest of the students?"

"We wanted to, but we were worried about Stacy." Nodding toward the ceiling to indicate the janitor's office upstairs, the armed girl said with her narrow eyes fixed on Miranda, "It was locked and we knocked on the door."

"One of the teachers in there had gotten free enough to talk to us."

Miranda sighed and shook her head, her eyes averting in disappointment. She had been pretty pleased by Luther's willingness to at least look to other people like he knew what he was doing in the middle of the firefight, but this was the last time she let him help her incapacitate hostages in any way. Always good to know what weaknesses you're going to have to balance in your life partner someday...

"I don't suppose they happened to tell you what way they planned to go when escaping through the ceiling?"

The girl without the gun almost looked ready to answer; the girl with it looked sharply at her and elbowed her in the ribs.

Miranda stepped toward her, still on the desk, and the girl fired her gun so near to Miranda's head that she swore she felt a hair sliced off.

As the bullets shattered the wall behind her, Miranda remained still. The girl ceased fire, looking shocked at herself. Her nostrils flared.

"Do you really think you could kill me, even if you had to?"

Miranda looked the girl in the eye, her hands still at either side of her head.

The gunwoman's lips trembled.

"If *Luther* can do it," she said after a few seconds, her expression hardening in spite of her tearful eyes, "I know I can."

"Luther hasn't killed anybody."

The girls laughed. The one with the gun fixed Miranda with a hateful stare and said, "You don't even know? I thought you were supposed to be his girlfriend."

Miranda looked blankly at the one pointing the rifle. "Tell me."

"People go missing around him. Just ask him. Everybody said it was just because he's bad luck, but after today? I think he must be, like, some kind of serial killer."

Unable to help herself, Miranda launched in. "Serial killers and mass murderers tend to exhibit very different pathologies, actually, though they are similar in many ways. They both crave attention, for one. For another, neither seems to suffer from the nightmares that afflict military veterans and other individuals suffering from Post-Traumatic Stress Disorder. Do you know what that is?"

The girl grit her teeth. Miranda went on.

"It's what happens when the brain endures extreme, unprocessable trauma. It's like a computer program that can't complete its task. The computer just keeps trying over and over to execute the same broken command, so it gets stuck in an infinite loop. The brain re-traumatizes itself, forever unable to cope with the reality of what happened. Of being a killer at the age of seven."

"I'm nine," corrected the girl softly, her eyes having drifted down to the gun in her hand. Her lips tightened. "But—this is self-defense."

"Is it? I'm unarmed. You should just keep me hostage and get an adult."

The girls exchanged a look, as if this should have been patently obvious to both of them from the start.

In reality, it was the most dangerous thing they could possibly choose to do.

While the one with the gun nodded to the doorway, Miranda took in the room one more time. About four feet to her left lay the remains of Roger's chair, the duct tape still attached and the blunt scissors abandoned in the disorder.

As the unarmed girl ran into the hall, Miranda locked eyes with the one foolish enough to remain.

"Now that we're alone, I can tell you the truth. You're going to die soon, so it doesn't matter."

The girl's eyes widened while Miranda went on.

"I did kill your friend. Stacy. Luther was there, but it isn't really his fault. I made it look like an accident... as much as anyone could, anyway.

"But you want to know what really happened?"

With the girl intent on an answer, Miranda took her chance and sprang from the desk with a hard kick aimed at the muzzle of the gun. It buried bullets in the floor until, upon landing, she knocked the other girl's out from under her. The hail thrashed along the ceiling until the girl lost her grip on the weapon.

The blunt scissors in her hand, Miranda pinned Stacy's friend down on the floor.

"I killed her on purpose," she said, "because I could tell that Luther liked her. And I will never feel bad about it."

While the girl screamed, Miranda raised the blunt scissors high and jammed them into fighting flesh. Stabbing was difficult with the old things, but not impossible.

It just meant that they hurt even more when jammed into the girl's screaming throat; her cheeks; against and through the palms of her fighting hands.

"No," screamed the girl, blood bubbling from her mouth as Miranda stabbed through her ribs, "no, no! Please!"

Miranda said nothing until the girl was silent.

With interloper incapacitated, Miranda got up and dusted off her dress, then fetched the gun.

She checked the clip with a frown and slapped it back in.

"I wish you hadn't wasted all that ammunition."

With a feather-light squeeze, Miranda spent one bullet in the girl's head.

It sounded like the AR-15 spit in her face.

With a deep sigh of relief to have one of the secondhand witnesses accounted for, Miranda spared an annoyed glance at the unplugged PC and charged after the other girl.

By the time Miranda emerged from the office, sneakers could be heard slapping on the concrete stairs to the next floor. Clearly the girl had delayed to think about intervening but chickened out. If Miranda had just emerged a few seconds sooner...

Cursing herself for taking too long, Miranda rushed after her prey and faintly hoped that Luther, already having dealt with his teachers, would be coming around the corner any minute.

She didn't expect it, though.

Strapping the gun around her neck and resolving not to let it go until she absolutely had to, Miranda darted toward the stairwell.

"Help! Help!"

The girl's screams only bolstered her pursuer's limbs. Miranda broke into a sprint worthy of an Olympic champion in her effort to keep the girl from releasing any information to any adults who still happened to be available.

The bees, however, seemed to have made short work of the SWAT. While Miranda emerged in the first floor of the museum, the girl's intensified screams received no response.

Miranda released a burst of rifle fire, leading the girl to let her run right into the bullets.

At the sound of the gun, the girl skidded to a halt sooner than Miranda had anticipated—or she tried to halt, anyway.

The same marbles that proved the undoing of the

SWAT team now claimed the life of the girl, who went skidding across the floor as marble on marble used her momentum to deliver her to doom. Screaming, Stacy's friend held out her hands to catch herself on the rail around the giant spirograph, but there was no stopping the machinations of fate.

Catapulting over the rail as a consequence of inertia, the girl smashed head-first into the paper wall proudly displaying previous giant spirographs. Her neck snapped while her brains splattered out in what was less a Pollock and more an explosion at the hardware store.

As a few pieces of brain tumbled down the wall and slid in lumps upon the base of the machine, Miranda lowered the gun.

Satisfied, she turned to leave and only stopped when something lured her to the main exhibit floor with a dying moan.

Double-checking the gun, Miranda cast a longing glance toward the basement steps and went to investigate.

And when she was through, she was going to be damn sure to lock the director's door behind her this time.

17

COLLEEN VIOLA WASN'T sure what was going on, but she just couldn't believe these innocent children were in any way at fault! While Colleen wiggled fruitlessly in her bonds, Bertha Johnson had succeeded in getting out of her gag even before the gunfire erupted in the lobby.

A good thing, too! Two of Mrs. Johnson's little angels came by, sent by God to help get the ladies out.

If only Mrs. Johnson would have a little more faith.

"We have to find our own way out before they come back," said the older woman grimly, wiggling across the concrete floor. The coordinated effort of her bound limbs looked a little like swimming. Slowly, inch by inch, Bertha managed to line herself up with Ms. Viola and lean in with her teeth.

"Praise the Lord," Colleen said with a gasp, working her lungs full of air denied them by the gag. "Oh, thank goodness you're still so spry, Bertha!"

"I'm barely forty," was Bertha's annoyed response. "Now, hold still."

While the older woman leaned down to gnaw on the bindings around Colleen's wrists, a full peal of gunfire rolled through the museum. Colleen's skin went clammy with fear.

"Don't you think we should just wait here until the kids go get us help, Bertha?"

"They're going to be *evacuated*," said Mrs. Johnson tersely, adding as she went back to her work, "and nobody's going to listen to what they have to say, anyway—not right now. Would you?"

Colleen imagined herself outside the building: trying to round up children, counting heads, figuring out how she was going to call parents, deciding whether to go in for any missing students.

"I guess you're right," said Colleen with a hefty sigh.

Saying nothing, Bertha only nodded.

It was a funny time for this, but Colleen felt a little bad about her misunderstanding Bertha's age. Maybe the confusion had arisen because Mrs. Johnson seemed so old-fashioned. Even her name was an old, old name, though it did seem to fit an austere sort of lady like her.

Colleen just couldn't relate to her coworker. She understood that Bertha was pragmatic, but there was pragmatic and then there was grim. Yes, there were a lot of very nice things about Bertha—she had a motherly way about her, and was awfully good with kids who didn't quite seem to fit in—but sometimes Colleen got the sense that Mrs. Johnson expected the worst out of life.

And you woulda thought bein' born in the Reagan administration would make somebody so optimistic!

Colleen, now. Colleen had seen her share of things, but she still managed to lift her head up high and look to the future. While Mrs. Johnson—and lots of other teachers, to be fair—fretted over the slow pace at which children learned to read these days, Ms. Viola tried to focus on the *positives*. For instance, sure! It was a shame that fewer parents seemed to regularly read with their kids, but on the flipside, it was pretty neat that kids were being taught coding at younger and younger ages! Wasn't it nice that society was settin' these little guys (*and* gals, of course!) up for a lifelong career in the cushy gray walls of a cubicle from the time they were in Pre-K?

Ms. Viola just thought that Mrs. Johnson was a little too liberal, if you really wanted to know the truth and could forgive her bringing up politics in mixed company. Bertha needed more faith in the status quo and its ability to overcome chaos.

"Look for something you can use to cut me free," Bertha pleaded, sitting up while Colleen separated her wrists and rubbed the raw portions. "We've got to find a way out of here."

"Oh, Birdie, honey"—that was what Colleen called Bertha, 'Birdie,' since it was easier on the tongue—"don't worry! The police have got to be on their way—heck, I'm sure they're probably *here* by now."

"If we just sit here and depend on the sheriff's office, we'll be done for."

Selecting a box cutter from the wall, Colleen hurried to Bertha's side just to make her calm. "The Good Lord wouldn't let a thing like that happen to us. Come on, Birdie! Have a little faith."

"God can't save us if we don't try to save ourselves," was Mrs. Johnson's response as she raised her arms toward Colleen. "Please, hurry."

"I'll try, hold still now—"

"Ah!"

In her rush to oblige her friend and slip the boxcutter into her bindings, Colleen managed to slide the fresh blade straight into the top few layers of Mrs. Johnson's skin. Her stomach lurched to see the little flap she'd managed to create when she slid the boxcutter back out, nausea tightening her stomach while the electricity of terror rushed down to the tips of her fingers.

"Oh, Birdie, I'm so sorry!"

"Never mind," Bertha said, hissing through clenched teeth. "Just hurry!"

Grimacing, feeling like if Birdie weren't rushing her she might not have made that mistake, Colleen went about more carefully cutting off the bindings around her friend's wrists. When those were away, she moved toward Mrs. Johnson's ankles—only to have the boxcutter snatched from her hand.

"I'll do it," said the older woman tersely, "thank you."

"Is your wrist okay, Birdie? I wonder if there are any bandages around here—"

"There's no time!"

Bertha sawed through her ankle ties as another round of gunfire tore through the lobby.

Then, another.

A firefight unfolded outside, unceasing. Both women glanced toward the sound.

Colleen's heart sank a little.

"You know," said Colleen softly, "maybe you're right. We really should get out of here. But how?"

"There's only one way," said Mrs. Johnson, tossing the remains of the cloth and old duct tape away from her legs before hurrying up the rungs of the ladder.

Colleen gasped, rushing to hold it for her.

"Don't do that, Birdie! You'll hurt yourself, those tiles are so weak!"

"They'll have to hold," said Bertha, shaking her head. "There's no choice. We just have to move fast."

Colleen bit her lip while her friend ascended the ladder and looked around the top of the drop ceiling.

At what point did the need to be polite become secondary to survival? Because, well...how could Colleen put this delicately...Bertha Johnson wasn't a *giant*, now, but she was a bigger lady. There was just no denying it. Colleen had no doubt the ceiling tiles would hold for *her*—but would they hold Bertha?

There was no time to ask. Driven by survival, Bertha dragged herself up over the edge of the tiles and disappeared from sight.

"How they holdin' up?"

Another round of gunfire was exchanged outside, this one even more intense. Pawing at her blouse, glancing over her shoulder at the doorway, Colleen clambered up the ladder after Birdie and peered over the edge.

Incredible! It was hard to see in the dim drop ceiling interior, but Birdie was showing some real hustle. You could hear it in the awful noises the flimsy brackets of the drop ceiling made with her movements. Tiles rattled and the thin aluminum swayed, but Mrs. Johnson had already managed to wiggle five tiles away and continued increasing the gap between herself and Colleen. As she made it as far as the partition between the janitor's office and the hallway just outside, Colleen tried touching the edge of the nearest tile.

The ladder wobbled beneath her. Crying out, feeling liable to fall any second, Colleen clutched the edge of the tile and hunched over to settle her light weight. A drop on the concrete would surely kill her. She shut her eyes and prayed.

Her meager influence over the ladder was registered after a few seconds, and she breathed a sigh of relief.

The explosion that rocked the building made her jump so sharply she unbalanced the ladder again, forced to endure the whole exercise over.

What in the hell was *that*? Good Lord, this was a nightmare!

While Mrs. Johnson disappeared into an uncomfortably maze-like corridor that seemed to follow along the areas around the lobby, Colleen bit her lip and forced herself to climb up into the tiles. She was shorter than Birdie and it took a little more momentum to slide from the rickety top of the folding ladder, but praise the Lord, she was able to scramble up by tossing her legs roughly upon the drop ceiling.

Able to breathe for the first time in a minute, Colleen applauded herself and looked around, impressed. This ceiling really was pretty high quality! Very impressive that it could keep its integrity against Birdie's weight.

She might have basked in it longer if the sound of footsteps approaching didn't give her pause.

Maybe she wouldn't have to crawl through the ceiling after all! Poor Birdie, doing all that work for nothing. This had to be the cops, right?

Still poised at the edge of the tile, Colleen strained her ears—ringing from the blast—and readied herself for the deep baritone of some heroic police officer. Maybe a nice, young, single man…her reward for enduring this. Everything happens for a reason, right, Lord?

The door flew open.

"Looks like we have to split up."

At the unexpected pitch of the girl's flat voice, everything flipped on its head.

Birdie had been right.

God wasn't going to save Colleen if Colleen wasn't going to save herself.

Heart racing, Colleen crawled into motion as quietly as she could. Since the janitor's office was apparently the room on this side of the building where the drop ceiling began, the only option was to follow Bertha.

As she shifted from one tile to another, Colleen was surprised and frightened by the relative instability of the drop ceiling. It had seemed response to Bertha's movements, but now that Colleen was up here, herself, the frame structure quivered beneath her body and the tiles which shifted ominously in their cradles. It aluminum seemed easily destabilized—more than she had expected.

Anxious, Colleen moved as smoothly as she could while still keeping the pace required to escape the children hunting for them below.

Good Lord! Where had Bertha gotten to? Colleen marveled that her friend had managed to get so far so fast without a problem. This ceiling wanted to wiggle everywhere, except the spots where there was a partition below. What a damn cheap science museum! Birdie was right. Nobody cared about education anymore.

Similarly, nobody cared about school shootings. It made Colleen sick with rage as she wiggled through the unstable ceiling. Somehow, no police had burst through the door to whisk her and Birdie away from peril. What the hell else were these damn bastard cops for?

Colleen's wiggling increased in speed when, too far behind her to see over her shoulder in the dark, the drop ceiling rattled with another body's weight. Ms. Viola rushed as much as rushing was possible when crawling through a dark drop ceiling, biting her lip as the tiles threatened to slide from place. Something wiggled against her arm and she repressed a shriek, letting her fright motivate her to move faster.

Then, the space changed.

The narrow corridor opened.

There were options.

The drop ceiling extended over the main exhibit floor.

Gasping, Colleen hurried to the far more open area, ignoring the access panel in the ceiling that she could just see Bertha pushing back into place behind her. Let her crawl around in the crummy crawlspaces all damn day long! Colleen was getting *out* of this death trap. The exhibit hall's rear had a set of glass doors that let out to a patio sculpture garden. If she could just find a safe place to drop down, she could rush out the back doors, surrender to the police, and check on her students.

She could go back to being a normal teacher, and continue living her life.

If only she hadn't crawled over the water-damaged section of tiles above the disassembled exhibit.

It were as though reality had begun operating on some sort of delay. Colleen put her hand straight through the tile and only realized she was falling forward through the flimsy aluminum when the water-damaged piece of polystyrene broke apart on the hard floor, shattering in all directions.

Gasping, Colleen twisted to grope for the drop ceiling's frame a second too late.

Like a diver springing into a pool, the screaming woman fell face-first onto a contrivance of plastic and metal making up the pieces of dissembled and somehow formless exhibit. A long pole exposed from the rest of the parts skewered the teacher, plunging into her cheek and slamming up to impale her body as gravity pulled her to her demise.

Shock raced to deaden Colleen to any understanding of what happened. Knowledge made it worse. It didn't matter what was wrong with her. She was still alive!

But as soon as she exerted effort to push herself up and away, the metal slorped back the way it had come. Blood flowed out of punctured organs.

Colleen gagged against the pain and stopped, unable to move further without killing herself and afraid that she already had.

Seemed like her policeman wasn't coming.

18

LUTHER COULDN'T FEEL his hands as he dragged himself into the drop ceiling to go after his teacher and her colleague.

As horrible as it was to think, he had really been hoping that Miranda would do this part of the job for him. Luther just wasn't the killing type. Once he had been mischievous, but certainly not violent. Then and now he didn't enjoy his teachers or school with any particular sincerity, but he didn't wish them any harm.

Still...at this point, with all the chaos that had unfolded and all the dead bodies piling up, Miranda was right. They couldn't let the witnesses live after everything that had happened.

Up ahead of him, one or both of the teachers scrambled to escape. What would he do once he cornered them? How would he corner *both* of them?

Would he actually be able to pull the trigger when he stared them down?

Miranda seemed to think nothing of it. Everything about this insane and disturbing day came effortlessly to her. He had to admit that she terrified him, but also brought with that terror a strange feeling of safety. Sort of like having a scary dog.

Or a scary wolf.

Where was Paine? What was he doing in the museum? Luther was starting to worry...especially after his comment about being useful. What a wolf considered useful and what a human considered useful were two very different types of useful.

What was it going to take to get Paine to understand that he couldn't live this way in domesticated society? Luther wasn't convinced there was *anything* that could be done. The wolf was an adult, accustomed to his lifestyle. The chaos he sowed around himself was a part of his personality.

Would it ever be possible for Luther to have the good parts of his friend without the really awful parts?

He just wasn't sure...and it hurt him terribly to think about, because Paine had always been there. They were like brothers; like a human and his shadow.

Another scream wracked the museum. Upon emerging from the corridor over the staff hallway and into a far vaster space, Luther peered through the dim for the source of the cry.

One of the tiles had fallen away toward a larger section of the floor, permitting light to flow in as though to mark a spot on a stage.

Stomach sinking, the boy edged toward it, mindful of weak portions of the drop ceiling.

At the edge of the tiles, he leaned over to see what lay beneath.

Luther wasn't sure what was more horrible: the twitching, convulsing body of Ms. Viola impaled on the metal of the dissembled exhibit, or the fact that he had accidentally peeked up her inverted skirt in the process of seeing her corpse.

Oh, well...guess it didn't really count anymore, since she was dead and all. Dead, or dying. A dead or dying woman just wasn't the same thing as a living woman. It wasn't even the same thing as a picture. It was more like looking at a wax sculpture, or an old mannequin.

In short...it was horrifying.

Leaning back with a shudder, Luther let himself have a few seconds of relief. One less kill to worry about.

Then, he turned back the way he came and caught sight of the blood he'd been following without even knowing it.

The hint of a blood trail was made clear to him by the light coming in from the fallen tile. It glistened from his new angle and crawled toward it, the AR-15 shifting on his back every inch of the way to remind him what he needed to do.

When he stopped before it, Luther realized the blood trail must have marked the teachers' entire path. It didn't follow Ms. Viola, though, instead continuing on past the point of her demise. Did Mrs. Johnson hurt herself in escaping her bindings? The fresh path clearly marked her exit through some kind of crawlspace access passage in the actual ceiling.

With a nervous glance down at the tiles beneath him, Luther removed the rifle to probe the door. Unlocked, unblocked, it gave way.

Soon, Luther was among all number of miscellaneous pipes, wires, and insulation lining the original ceiling of the building. The boy had to move carefully to avoid taking away a splinter from the exposed beams around, especially since the darkness here was almost complete. At the very least, as long as he stooped, the slight height of the crawlspace made it possible for Luther to walk rather than crawl.

So, hunched halfway over, Luther rushed after the teacher whose breaths he heard in the dark. She was still far off, her footsteps betraying her presence with creaking boards and the clap of clog-like shoes.

And when they turned the corner one after the other, she almost cried out to see what she thought was a dead-end.

Luther had thought she had seen some kind of rat or cockroach and braced himself for a hideous surprise. Instead, he came around the corner just as Mrs. Johnson, after thinking herself at a dead-end for a few seconds, found the latch of a door.

The gasping teacher threw open the rooftop exit and hurried into the blazing sunlight.

On hand lifting, Luther winced against the inundation of sunlight before surging after her.

The boy barely waited to get out of the crawlspace before firing after the teacher, who ran, screaming. She had made it halfway across the roof and could have gone on longer, but a bullet ricocheted off the concrete near her foot.

Mrs. Johnson yelped, leaping away and, in the process, twisting her ankle. The teacher fell to the roof like a sack of potatoes and Luther did his best to ignore the impulse to apologize to her.

"Stop," she cried. "Stop, please—"

Well...what was the harm in apologizing? "I'm sorry, Mrs. Johnson. There's just no other way."

"But *why*? Why are you doing this?"

"Because...otherwise, I'll get in too much trouble. My life will be over, and I'm still trying to—I just want to be a kid."

"But you don't have to be in trouble! If you let me live—let everyone live—maybe the courts could be easy on you. They're reasonable. They would understand you're sick."

The boy's lips twisted in annoyance. "I'm not *sick*. Please, Mrs. Johnson, don't make this hard."

"It *should* be hard," she told him, her tone chiding. "It should be the hardest thing you've ever done, killing another person. There shouldn't be anything easy about it and I'm not going to *make* it easy."

Luther glanced down at the gun in his hands, then at his shoes. "I know you must think I'm horrible, but—I just don't know what else to do."

"You're a good boy, Luther! You don't have to do anything like this. There are options."

Luther shook his head.

"Yes there are," Mrs. Johnson told him in a tone that begged him to agree.

'No, Mrs. Johnson." Luther shook his head more rapidly and told her, "That's not what I mean."

While the teacher's talking hands fell to her sides to brace her upon the concrete, Luther said softly, "I'm not a good boy. My friend, Paine, is the only one who really knows what I'm like. Everybody thinks I'm weird, or even bad. I *want* to be good. I want to be normal." Just trying to broach this subject with an adult who wouldn't be around much longer was almost too much to bear. Luther wiped one hand across his eyes, saying sincerely, "He won't let me."

"Paine won't? Your wolf?"

Luther nodded.

"But—"

"And now you're going to tell me that Paine isn't real," said Luther, forcing back the tears and making himself raise his eyes toward his teacher. "Now you're going to feel bad for me and tell me it's all in my head. You'll say I *am* sick. That I'm seeing things, or maybe just that I'm confused. You'll tell me I can see a doctor.

"But Paine is real. He's one hundred percent real, and he can hurt people. He *has* hurt people."

Slowly coming to terms with the inescapable reality of her situation, Mrs. Johnson studied Luther grimly. "Who has Paine hurt?"

"My babysitter," said Luther sadly, "and one of my mom's friends, though *she* survived. And there was even one time where he said—where he started thinking about maybe eating my mom, too. That's why I had to start taking him to school every day, see—I can't leave him alone in my house. I don't know what he'll do to my parents."

"Luther," said Mrs. Johnson softly, her conciliatory tone of no use to him now.

The body of his babysitter, her organs wet and red and chewed in the woods, came rushing back to him. For a few seconds he fancied his hands were still sticky with their blood; that his mother still wanted to know when the babysitter left him alone that night, and demanding how he got so much dirt under his nails.

"I didn't know what else to do, see. I had to protect my mom by taking him to school—especially because, whenever Paine does something bad, I'm the one who gets blamed for it. That's why I had to help him with Olivia. Instead of taking the blame...I helped him get rid of the evidence. He ate her; and once he was finished eating her, I helped him bury the bones and clothes and things. We took them deep into the woods in my red wagon, and—and—"

Luther's lips trembled. Mrs. Johnson looked at him in silence, horrified and saddened.

"I *want* to be good, Mrs. Johnson," blubbed Luther, rapidly wiping his cheeks with one dirty hand again. "I really do. And I want my parents to think I'm good, because I don't know if they'd love me otherwise... but I love my friend, too. He's my best friend. And...I don't know what I'd do without him."

Weeping—frantic, almost cartoonish—echoed through the roof.

Luther almost thought it was his own until Paine stepped out of the shadows of the nearby water tank, blowing his nose on a handkerchief he tucked back into his fur.

For the first time all day, Luther knew everything would be all right.

While the boy straightened up, crying with joy, "Paine!" the wolf placed a great paw over his fuzzy heart.

"Oh, Luther! That was really beautiful. I love you, too. What would I do without a friend like you?"

Mrs. Johnson's eyes bugged from her head at the sight of the gangly wolf.

"What in God's name—"

Whipping toward the old lady with a savage growl,

Paine let his ears pin back and said darkly, "Do you *mind*? We're trying to have an emotional reunion here. Oh, jeez—now look what you've done! You've blown it."

A snarl peeled past the wolf's lips.

Mrs. Johnson screamed and struggled to her feet while the beast sprang upon her.

Luther cried out, turning his face away as his teacher's desperate pleas for help transfigured to the wet rasps of torn vocal chords. While the wolf tore open her blouse and then her flesh to slurp up her glistening pink jelly-fat along with all the offal he could stand, the boy clapped his hands over his ears.

Still, he heard too much.

It was better than killing her himself, at least...but not by all that much.

By the time the wolf decided she was dead and he was satisfied, the megaphones had once again started up around the building.

"Sheriff Hayward? Are you still in there?"

Licking the digits of his bloody paw, the wolf emitted a crude belch. As Luther wrinkled his nose, Paine said, "Phew! I hope you kids can take care of anybody that's left, because I'm running out of room! Anyway, where were we...oh, yeah—"

With huge eyes for the big, blood-covered wolf that swept toward him, Luther said, "Paine! Not here—"

Too late! Tail wagging, his rancid breath smelling of raw meat and perforated bowel with every kiss he delivered, Paine snatched the boy up into a stifling embrace that left him sputtering—and relieved.

At the familiar fur of his friend, all the ugliness and horror went away. Sure, this wolf covered in blood had just murdered his teacher...but it was only so Luther didn't have to do it, himself.

Tears of gratitude welling in his eyes, Luther returned his friend's embrace.

"I love you, Paine," he told the towering wolf, who swung the boy around a bit before setting him down upon his feet. "Don't ever leave me alone, okay?"

"Not for any longer than I have to, kid."

With a ruffle of Luther's hair and a happy smile, the wolf straightened up and put his hands on his hips. One ear twitched as the megaphones carried on.

"Roger Garnet—if you can hear us, please verify the whereabouts of Sheriff Hayward." The lieutenant's unconvincing tone had a little warble to it; Pain's muzzle quirked up in a smirk. "If you cannot confirm that he is still alive and cannot provide a phone for him to call out to us to prove his welfare, we will have no choice but to make a re-enter the museum."

"How embarrassing!" Shaking his head, Paine nodded the boy toward the door that let them back into the crawlspace. "Usually you only want to do that *once* when you're sieging a place. Well, let's hurry up and get out of here. Where'd you leave your little pal?"

Gunshots rang out from somewhere in the museum.

"Oh," said the wolf brightly as Luther rushed ahead, "that's where!"

19

SHERIFF HAYWARD'S DAY just kept getting better.

Yes, he was being sarcastic.

Since violent death in Smokeland was nearly unheard of, the vast majority of the force on-duty had congregated in and around the Krumb house. Suddenly even beat cops who should have been walking around downtown to keep vagrants from sitting on benches too long were members of the homicide squad.

Sort of miraculous. Who was handing out all these promotions?

As a consequence, everybody milling around the Krumb place had to be rallied and divided for the matter of the shooting. On the one hand it was convenient, because proximity allowed for two officers to immediately show up at the museum and help secure the area, blockade traffic, and evacuate the building.

On the other hand, those officers were basically less than useless. With the rest of the cops in town fleeing to the station to gear up, the lieutenant and sergeant who showed up at the museum each had nothing but the pistols on their hips and the uniforms on their backs.

In other words—once the main floor of the museum seemed clear at a glance, Sheriff Hayward got the fuck away from those doors.

Just in the nick of time, too, it would sound from the sudden inundation of gunfire that came from within not moments later.

Outside, people wept and held each other and tried poorly to coordinate some explanation of what happened. A few adults congregated by the bushes, watching as SWAT members pulled up one van at a time. The Sheriff picked on this group of faculty first, chasing a group of kids off to the other side of the parking lot and telling the frantically whispering grown-ups, "I'm gonna need you folks to tell me everything you can think to tell me, right now. Are you with the museum, or the schools?"

"I'm with the museum," said a lady with glasses, "and so is he, and these two are parent chaperones."

"Are there any teachers around? Somebody who knows all the kids, or who has a class list?"

"We were just discussing that," said a portly chaperone, a mother whose wispy locks of dyed red hair kept slapping across her forehead in the breeze. "I don't see either of our teachers around."

"There were three different groups from three different schools coming today," said the administrator, taking her phone from her pocket. "One of them seems to be accounted for, but as for the teachers from the other schools…"

While the sheriff hovered over her shoulder, she pulled up her work e-mail and scrolled through it to the field trip registration forms. "Mrs. Carraway from Runner Elementary here in town, and two other teachers from a few towns away…here they are, Bertha Johnson and Colleen Viola."

"And they're not anywhere out here that you can see?"

The young woman looked grimly up at the sheriff and shook her head.

Sighing, Sheriff Hayward removed his hat and rubbed his forehead for a few long seconds.

"I sure would have appreciated it if you would have told me just about anything else," he answered at last, setting his hat back atop his head. "May I have a word with you two museum employees in private for a few seconds?"

After luring them to the foot of a climbing wall, a spot near enough to the front of the museum that Hayward could keep an ear on the situation, the sheriff looked between them and said, "What can you tell me about Roger Garnet?"

The unfortunate truth was that they couldn't deliver a whole lot more than Hayward already knew. Garnet was a transplant, a loner whose personal life was fairly unknown but whose professional record, so far as the museum knew, was impeccable. A little depressed and distant since his divorce. Definitely the type to shoot up a public place.

So when the SWAT was organized a few minutes later, and, shortly thereafter, Sheriff Hayward got a call patched through from inside of the museum, he was willing to give Garnet some kind of break.

But that call changed things. The threats were clear, especially amid all the gunfire and explosions. Roger Garnet was obviously hoping that the police would come in and take the responsibility for his life out of his hands. He wanted them to kill him.

And if that was what Hayward had to do to stop this sick son of a bitch from taking any more lives, then by God, he would be glad to do it.

The sheriff had to admit, however...even he was losing faith in the police force's capacity to do its job. Cops were either too soft or too sadistic, and that was just a fact of modern living. People got into the job for the wrong reasons. He thought he had better men, but that opinion changed in the museum. As the SWAT flailed before him, at a loss as to how to overcome a few fuckin' bees, Sheriff Hayward wondered if he was the only cop left who gave a good goddamn about protecting and serving anything but his own interests.

So, while the team bailed out amid piles of red welts that swiftly began to blossom along cheeks and lips, Sheriff Hayward grabbed an abandoned rifle, made sure his pistol was accessible to him in his belt, and plunged through the panicking officers whose discipline he was already planning.

And wouldn't you know it?

Made it all the way to the staff door without getting stung.

The door itself was stuck, but not locked. Sheriff Hayward shoved against it while keeping the handle held down. Slowly but surely, the thing gave; Hayward scoffed to find that a tipped-over roll of blue plastic was the only thing between him and Roger Garnet.

Well...a roll of blue plastic, and the grisly cadaver of a woman who, Sheriff Hayward couldn't help but guess, was one of the teachers missing from the parking lot.

With a scoff, Hayward shut the door behind him and did the decent thing that Garnet was in too much of a hurry to do. The sheriff unrolled the blue tarp and draped it over the teacher, making a mental note of her location for later scrutiny.

The staff hallway was wide and long and, so far as Hayward could tell, wrapped around quite a bit of the museum to allow access to various storage and equipment rooms without getting onto the main floor. Garnet's options for escape were limited, and since he hadn't been stupid enough to use one of the emergency exits out of the building and into the waiting arms of the officers stationed around the exterior, he had probably continued on running through the hall to some other exit door.

But where in the museum would he exit?

Hayward flipped on his flashlight and hurried down the hallway in hot pursuit of any kind of sign.

Damn.

He'd hoped that there would be some kind of blood trail from where Garnet massacred that poor teacher, footprints or the like...and there were plenty off in the distance, enough to confirm he was going the right direction.

But, between Sheriff Hayward and those tracks Garnet couldn't help but leave, a long, slick trial of blood and organs marked the effortless way the woman had been disemboweled and dragged about fifteen yards down the hall. A grown-ass woman, mind, who was in fine shape but still some real trouble to move around while fightin' and screamin' and hollarin', as any cop who has ever detained a small female suspect may have been surprised to discover.

This Garnet guy must have been one hell of a fight. Hayward followed his steps grimly, braced for the battle of his life.

It just never occurred to the sheriff that he might *lose* that life.

Somehow—somehow, after all the risks, all the calculated gambles, all the times he had *not* died, Sheriff Hayward just took for granted that he *wouldn't* die. He had grown jaded by a career that was at once too easy, yet not what he was promised it would be when he was a young man and the world seemed so different.

It was not so much that Sheriff Hayward carried delusions of immortality so much as that he had become to his sense of status quo, which for him was a his daily alive-ness. He was a bit overweight, but he had no ailments other than occasional heartburn and a thinning hairline; he was the sort of driver who hadn't had a ticket since he was seventeen, and who hadn't been involved in an accident since a fender bender of his parents' where he was in the car; he went to the doctor for his physical every year and never skipped a booster shot; he'd even quit smoking twenty years before and never looked back.

Sheriff Hayward was a good, conscientious, healthy man, and because he was those things, he felt he was doing his part. It was natural to him that reality would therefore fulfill its half of the bargain and provide him with that long, happy life he was owed. He had a sense of entitlement toward existence that could not be shaken.

Even though—or almost because—he saw it all the time, Hayward had lost touch with the reality that death could come at any time, in any form; and that when it was a man's time, that was just the way things were.

Garnet's aptly-colored trail led Hayward around the corner and down the central staff hall. Was this one of two wings? It seemed to terminate sooner than expected, along with Garnet's footprints.

Three doors lined this end of the hall. Storage rooms of various kinds, based on checklists hung on the wall beside each door.

One was for more general school supplies; one was dangerous chemicals; and one was labeled as a workshop.

Garnet's footprints led to all three of 'em, and out to the main exhibit hall.

Trying to be clever, the sheriff guessed.

With his gun low, Hayward burst into the storage room of school supplies and confirmed it was empty. Really, he spared little more than a glance and a quick sweep around the door to make sure Garnet wasn't hiding in a corner.

Shutting it behind him, Garnet pressed to the wall. The next door was a potentially deadly one; who knew what chemicals a science museum had to have on-hand for demonstrations?

Hayward kicked the door open and scanned the shelves, looking for any sign of Garnet.

Nothing but a bunch of glass jars marked with warning stickers. Compressed gas for various pieces of equipment. Batteries. Some gigantic metal container on wheels that bore a caution label declaring its contents to be liquid nitrogen.

Finding nothing, Sheriff Hayward stepped back from the storage room just in time to keep Garnet from getting the drop on him.

Because he was ready for anything, Hayward managed to dodge most of the liquid nitrogen splashing from the dewar in Garnet's hands—but he just couldn't escape all of it.

As the boiling liquid splashed across his skin, Hayward screamed to watch his own hand release the AR-15's front half. While the rifle swung down, Garnet took his chance to drop the metal container and grab the weapon in his thickly gloved hands.

Hayward fired randomly, a burst of bullets gatling out into Roger's shin and the floor around.

While the director released the sheriff's weapon with a howl of pain, Hayward shook his burning hand and did his best to ignore it while regaining control. Limping as fast as he bled, Garnet disappeared into the workshop and shut the door.

There was no time to waste. Gun at the ready, saving words for later, Hayward slammed the door open and just managed to duck the burst of gunfire from within.

While bullets tore holes in the painted bricks of the staff corridor, Sheriff Hayward pressed himself to the wall alongside the door and waited for a break in the storm. It came only a few seconds later, during which time he lowered the AR-15 and unholstered his far more trustworthy handgun.

"I'm not the one you should be trying to shoot," Garnet whined. "Do you hear me out there? I'm telling you, I'm not behind this."

"Uh-huh. Who was it that killed that nice teacher back there, then?"

"It was the wolf! I can't believe nobody's seen it but me—Deborah must have seen it before it killed her."

"Wolf, huh?"

"Christ—you don't believe me, either."

That was one way of putting it. Garnet was off his rocker and, like most crazy people, sensitive about it.

Hayward pulled back the hammer of the gun. "Now, I ain't sayin' I don't believe you saw what you saw. I'm just wondering how a wolf fires a rifle, 'r throws a hand grenade."

"That wasn't *me*," Garnet protested, caught up enough in his pleas that he was unprepared for Hayward to duck around the corner and fire.

Crying out, Garnet dropped the battered rifle and raised his hands.

Hayward laughed.

"First sensible thing you've done all day! Stay right where you are."

The gun held before him, Hayward slowly approached and slid his non-dominant hand down to pluck the handcuffs from his belt. "Roger Garnet, I am placing you under arrest for the murder of several teachers and students, as well as the destruction of the science museum. You have the right to remain silent—"

Though he wasn't as strong as the teacher's blood smear implied, Garnet moved fast. Hayward had almost snapped the cuffs when the suspect dropped to the ground like a lead weight and grabbed the cop's gun as he did.

Desperate to keep hold on the weapon, Hayward went down with him and wrestled all the way.

The workshop was considerably larger than the other two back rooms, which was perhaps the only reason Garnet had space to wiggle away from Sheriff Hayward and finally knock the gun from his hand with his new vantage. While Hayward reached for the flying gun, Roger clenched a fist and punched him right in the face.

The sheriff saw stars, his eyes watering as the director stumbled up and yanked the rifle from his neck. Hayward grabbed him by the ankle and brought him down again, cursing as the rifle flew even farther away than the handgun. His hand searched for the handcuffs in the fog of war and found nothing. When he turned his attention to the gun instead, Garnet kicked the ever-loving shit out of Sheriff Hayward's burned hand. With a hiss of pain, the sheriff let go but stumbled up after his quarry and overtook him before he had reached the door.

"Where the hell's everybody runnin' to today? I remember a time when a man would be humiliated to act the way ya'll have today...then again, real men wouldn't murder children."

"I'm telling you! It's not—"

Savoring the opportunity to do so, Sheriff Hayward smashed Garnet's head against the door and threw him back into the depths of the room.

He was sick of this shit. So help him, he had been convinced for a few seconds of this encounter that he could talk Garnet down...but it seemed less and less likely every second, and less desirable, too.

It just really pissed him off to think of this wheedling little shit trying to be a big man by being a murderer.

"You know, Garnet, I's gonna arrest you above-board and all...but now I think I'm just gonna grant your wish."

Charging to the table saw where Garnet had caught himself and now stumbled to his feet again, Hayward threw a punch in the back of the bastard's head. Garnet cried out satisfyingly.

And Hayward would have thrown another if Garnet hadn't slammed on the saw at just the right time.

While the blade whined into fast, vicious motion, its cruel teeth a perfect blur like one great beast, Garnet turned just enough to catch Hayward's neck punch. The suspect cried out at the impact against the sheriff's hand. One hand braced against the sheriff's elbow while Garnet cringed away.

And in his effort to push the sheriff's arm away, Garnet swung Hayward's forearm right into the whirring saw.

Sheriff Hayward watched his own flesh split off from muscle and shining pink bone with the same awe shown by Garnet, who looked as though he were totally mystified by the wound. As the sheriff cried out in horror and an agony like nothing he'd experienced, he managed to dislodge his arm and the flap that was still hanging by a thread. The bloody blade of the table saw whirled on while the sheriff fell upon the floor and thrashed around, gasping for air. For a few seconds, the pain was too great for him to even think of reaching for his gun.

Garnet stood there, his stupor long and reminiscent of schizophrenia.

All the sheriff knew next was that the suspect disappeared.

Sweat pouring down his brow, his entire arm on fire, his eyes averting to and from the flopping wound jetting more and more blood across the floor all the time, Sheriff Hayward got it together enough to push himself toward the gun with his trembling legs.

His unwounded arm extended.

His fingers brushed the metal.

Hayward wrapped his fist around the handle of the gun and wondered, as Roger's footsteps marked his return to the room, how the fuck he was supposed to even aim the thing.

He would have no choice.

Hayward lifted his head, the gun trembling in his hand.

With the liquid nitrogen rolling behind him and a metal hose held in his gloved hand, Roger took advantage of the sheriff's raised head. The hose got crammed so far into Hayward's mouth that he gagged, the back of his throat pounded by the cold tip seconds before the liquid nitrogen went pouring in.

The first thing Sheriff Hayward knew was that the jamming, gagging sensation in the back of his throat evolved into an uncontrollable gag reflex that caused his body to rapidly and compulsively vomit. Strictly speaking, this was the right move to avoid consuming the liquid nitrogen—but when it came to the consumption of a fluid that boiled at -320 degrees Fahrenheit, a little went a long way.

Hayward's body was forcing him to vomit back up against the hose as rapidly as it could, but with nowhere for either the puke or the liquid nitrogen to go, both gradually made their way back down. As what little was successfully forced around the outer edges of the funnel burned his cheeks with both bile and chemicals, the rest burned his throat so horribly he weakly screamed through freezing vocal cords. It felt as though he were drinking boiling water.

He might as well have been.

While his entire esophagus burned with a pain more urgent than any he'd ever felt, Hayward fired off the gun and found he was easily foiled. Swatting the weapon away, Garnet opened the valve to let the chemical flow faster.

Hayward's weakened hand dropped to the floor along with the gun it held. The burning had become so intense that everything inside of him was numb, save for the awful cramps that threatened to rupture his stomach while the liquid vaporized into a gas amid his internal body temperature. While his clothes went tight against his expanding stomach, his chest seemed to tighten, too. Everything burned beyond belief.

Two things happened at once. As his freezing internal organs were ruptured by the expanding gas, a brew of shit and blood began to violently fill the cop's trousers.

At least he couldn't smell it, because he was also asphyxiating.

Unable to bear the putrid stench of a man shitting out his own stomach lining, Garnet dropped the hose, stumbled away from the thrashing sheriff, and plucked up a jingling set of keys from somewheres in the room.

While Hayward's uniform at last lost buttons to the expansion of his stomach, the bulging-eyed man tried to scream.

He could not even get a breath in to do it, his blue face and bursting eyes looking as though death was already upon them.

When his stomach and bowels ruptured his inflated torso and sent an explosion of organ meats splattering in all directions, it finally was.

20

THE SMOKELAND SCIENCE museum had become an orchestra pit of misery. Miranda followed the mysterious groan that punctuated the elimination of Stacy's friends and, gun still in her hands, emerged in the main exhibit hall.

Sacrificed within a ritual circle of caution tape, one of Luther's teachers twitched occasionally upon the dissembled exhibit that had drawn the disapproval of the director only earlier that day. Miranda glanced up at the ceiling, nodded at the gap in the tiles, and put the teacher out of her misery with a rifle shot to the head.

A terrible bellow arose from one of the two staff doors at the back of the exhibit hall.

Perking, Miranda rushed through the vaulted room and pressed herself against the metal door.

Machinery of some kind ran on the other side, grinding away while the grew worse.

Was that a table saw?

Her morbid curiosity—or, as she would say, her curiosity—getting the better of her, Miranda cracked open the door and peered into the staff hall beyond.

Another tile dropped out of the ceiling and Miranda whipped her rifle toward it, her fascination with the noises forgotten.

She only relaxed when the shadow that leapt down with a boy in its arms wagged its tail at her.

"Paine," she said in relief, lowering her weapon. "Luther. Did you finish the other one?"

"All taken care of," answered Paine brightly, setting the boy upon his feet and flashing a brilliant doggy smile. "How about you?"

"I've fallen behind," answered Miranda. "I had an interruption I needed to take care of."

Luther looked at her warily. "What kind of interruption?"

"There are still two adults who need to be eliminated," said Miranda, ignoring her friend's nervous question. "Roger Garnet, and my teacher, Mrs. Carraway."

"Teacher, huh? What's she smell like?"

While the wolf sniffed the air, the girl answered, "Cheap perfume."

"That doesn't narrow it down too much in this place, with all those chaperones...say—she's not a redhead, is she?"

"So you *have* seen her?"

"*Seen* her! If she's the dame I'm thinking of, she was delicious!"

While the wolf laughed and Miranda could at last breathe with relative ease, Luther whipped his head toward his friend.

"How many people have you *killed* today?"

"Oh, only…" Pausing to count off on his claws, Paine thought it through and answered, "I mean, just three if you include the golf ball thing."

Luther's brow furrowed. As Miranda's ears perked to note the staff hallway screams hand come to a stop, the boy pressed his hand to his forehead. "Will it always be like this? Does it *have* to always be like this?"

"Ah, kiddo, come on! Don't go feelin' bad. I thought we settled this when I killed Mrs. Johnson for you."

For a half a second, the boy's angry look sustained itself. When it ironed out to sorrow, his voice had softened.

"I'm glad I didn't have to do it on my own on the roof up there, but I wish—I just wish things were different."

Paine's ears drooped.

"I don't mean anything by it, Luther."

"I know, Paine—but—"

The boy squeezed his eyes shut, a sad little noise working its way up his throat.

"I can't keep *doing* this for you. Helping you— covering for you. Taking the blame for you."

Looking annoyed, Paine asked, "I'm helping *you* here. And what else are we supposed to do? Am I supposed to sit there, inert forever? Ignoring my every natural impulse? An *actual* stuffed animal?"

"No," said Luther quickly, while Miranda fought the onset of her own annoyance.

Now was not the time for this. As a repulsive series of flatulent reverberations emanated from the same location as the prior screams, Miranda shut the staff door all the way and turned to face her friends.

"Is it a wolf's instinct to walk on his hind legs?"

Paine and Luther both looked at her, the former somewhat baffled. His ears twitched as he asked, "What?"

"Talking? Is that part of being a wolf, too? I wasn't aware."

"Well—"

"And living with a kid while pretending to be a stuffed animal? They must have left that out of the nature documentary I watched a few years ago."

"Yeah," Paine tried to defend, "but—"

"It would seem to me that you do quite a few things contrary to the instincts of a traditional wolf. Why can't you eat your meals politely instead of killing people for them, since you're distinguished in all these other ways?"

While Luther, his eyes ringed with hope, mouthed the words, "Thank you," Paine's lips twisted over his muzzle in a cartoonishly annoyed scowl.

"Can't I have *one* thing in my life that's natural?"

"But you're *not* natural, are you, Paine?" Her tone as level with him as her eyes strove to be across their varied heights, Miranda stared Paine down (or up) and said, "You're some kind of demon—an old trickster god, like Coyote or Anansi...or something unmentionable that humans would categorize as such, anyway."

The so-called wolf looked taken aback. After his muzzle had hung open for a few seconds, his lips folded back broadly from his glittering fangs.

"Wouldn't you say a trickster god is natural? A force of nature, anyway."

"Then you should consider less lethal tricks in the future. Aside from the fact that leaving witnesses alive will leave more people who can remember being tricked by you and therefore increase your power by recognition, sooner or later, your antics will get Luther put in jail."

Paine's tail drooped sincerely at that thought, his ears following suit. The wolf's dark eyes trailed toward the boy.

Miranda nodded once, glad Paine's affection for Luther was genuine as such a creature's affection could be.

She could relate to that, after all.

"What will you do then, Pain?" She went on digging into the weakness, gesturing to Luther. "Where will you stay? Who will witness your existence—especially those compassionate and miraculous tricks, of which I am sure you are equally capable?"

Paine's lips pursed while the boy looked hopefully up at him.

Shifting the gun to one side, Luther extended his hand.

Paine took it, holding it there for a few seconds before his ears twitched and his expression grew firm with urgency.

"Hide," commanded the wolf, whisking Luther up and stuffing him behind a nearby exhibit on centrifugal force.

Miranda rushed along with them, her AR-15 at the ready and her body tense.

The staff door open.

Roger Garnet stepped out.

The last hour or so had not been kind to anyone in Smokeland, but Garnet looked especially altered by his day. His wrinkled, blood-covered polo shirt was painted in the same grit and gore that lined his cheeks. The lines in his forehead had cut creases through the mask of read and it made him look like a pitiful clown: like a tenor at the end of Pagliacci, ready to go home and go to bed. Those eyes, though, went unseeing out well over a thousand yards, his pupils so massive with mushrooms that Miranda had to wonder if he was even fully aware of the consequences of his actions.

With a glance at Luther, Paine jerked into movement.

Miranda grabbed his forearm, ignoring the slight growl that Garnet seemed not to notice.

In fact, it would seem Garnet didn't notice anything.

A trail of blood in his wake, Garnet made his slow way across the exhibit hall.

"Let's see where he goes," she whispered. "I have a hunch."

Garnet was a troublesome patsy because, whether he realized it was Miranda behind all of this or not, by now he *realized* he was a patsy. Therefore, as a patsy, Garnet's number one goal would be to clear his name and prove he had nothing to do with the terrible destruction at the Smokeland Science Museum that day.

The easiest way to prove his innocence?

Show somebody the security camera footage from the science museum.

On the tips of their toes, the children and the wolf crept quietly after Garnet. The final witness to the bacchanalia of their crimes wandered listlessly through the main hall of the museum, the weapon in his hands seared and dented so that it looked like a toy. Must have been that bully's.

Sure enough, Garnet wove and wobbled to the basement stairs.

It was perfect. They just had to time things properly—to get in there and kill Garnet just after he had logged in. The process would be faster than trying to crack the computer from a dead start.

"You have five more minutes to furnish proof of Sheriff Hayward's wellbeing or face the consequences, Garnet. Release the sheriff and come out with your hands up!"

And they were going to *have* to be fast.

Garnet shared their sense of haste, fortunately. With his own life on the line just as much or even more than theirs, the director of the science museum scrambled into action to move the desk back into place and plug the computer in. The children listened while the wolf crouched beside them in the hallway.

"Come on," Garnet whispered to himself, "Come on..."

The hum of electronics; the rapid tick-tack of typing, followed by a strangled noise, followed by more typing.

Miranda waited, the soft clicking of the mouse intermittent at first.

"You have three minutes."

"Yes," whispered Garnet.

Rifle at the ready, Miranda burst into the room.

"Hands up—step away from the computer."

Though he cried out, Garnet whipped around with the rifle in his hands and, much to Miranda's surprise, actually fired.

Suffice it to say, Miranda should have been more prepared. Garnet had been pushed past any reasonable limit of decent behavior. Given what he had gone through—and the inciting incident that had begun it when his intimate moment with Deborah was interrupted—the ease with which he shot at a child was not surprising.

That lack of surprise didn't stop Luther from crying out.

Even Miranda, she would have had to admit, gave a little shriek—though that was only due to the force with which Paine knocked her out of the line of fire.

While her rifle flew out of her hands, Luther aimed his.

Garnet's wild eyes grew wilder as his shoulder jerked back behind a bullet spray.

Gun still in his hand, he fell back at just the right angle to slam the his head on the corner of the desk.

Silent as death, Garnet fell, bleeding, upon the floor.

Relieved, Miranda nodded to Paine before springing up to check the computer.

They'd come in at the right time. The security program was open to the streams for the day, all of which was being backed up to an online server. Miranda set about erasing data both locally and in the cloud while Luther trembled.

"Oh, no—I killed him."

"You saved me," Miranda said. "I owe you my life."

"That doesn't mean he deserved to lose his."

"Ah, buddy...come here."

Folding his arms around the kid, Paine patted his friend and wagged his tail. Almost on contact, Luther succumbed to the tears that had waited all morning. Miranda spared a brief glance of pity for the sensitive boy as she hurried through the prompts that confirmed she meant to delete the files she had selected.

Upstairs, amid militaristic screaming, more glass and steel burst apart.

"You better hurry," urged Paine frantically. "We've got to go."

"There."

Breathless, Miranda slammed the final key and double-checked her work.

Everything was gone: not a frame of footage existed of the day.

Satisfied, the girl turned back to her friends. "Let's go. Put that gun down, Luther. We can't be seen with it."

Nodding, the boy slid the weapon from his shoulders and dropped it to the floor with a look of absolute derision for it, as though it were a snake that had bitten his mother.

Feeling the sparkling release of a true crisis evaded, Miranda grabbed his hand and pulled him toward freedom.

Garnet's warped M16 clicked as he readied it to fire.

Typical...that head wound had looked fatal, but Garnet was so hopped up on adrenaline and endorphins that, the psilocybin aside, he probably could have wrestled an alligator while actively dying.

And, based on the glistening hint of reddish brain-jelly visible amid the bloody crevice of his scalp, he was indeed actively dying—but not fast or definitively enough for Miranda's taste.

"Hold on there," he said, his words slow and measured but still comprehensible. "You're not going...anywhere."

"What are you going to do? Hand us over to the cops?" Miranda looked at him pointedly, her hands visible even though Garnet aimed the weapon at the wolf. "Sorry to tell you this, but your evidence is gone."

"I don't care about—*exoneration*." Tears filling his eyes, Garnet looked between the children and spared special disdain for the boy who regarded his shoes. "You killed me! You killed me...and for what?"

Miranda shrugged. "To look in the janitor's office."

Balking, trying to make sense of this through his bleeding brain, Roger asked, "But—don't you have *any* regard for human life?"

"Of course," answered Miranda blandly. "I love life. And I love death, too."

"You're sick. All three of you are sick."

Tears streaming down his cheeks, Roger pointed the gun at Miranda and said, "The only ones who deserve to die today are *you*."

Just like before, it was Paine who saved Miranda— and this time, he grabbed Luther, too.

"Hold on!" The wolf swept a kid up in each forepaw while he ducked out of the room with a yelp for his tail, caught in the gunfire. "Yowza!"

"Paine! Are you okay?"

At Luther's cry, the wolf bent forward and tossed the kids upon his back. While they each clutched a fistful of fur, Luther clinging to the beast's neck and Miranda tightening her legs beneath fuzzy ribs, Paine rolled into a gallop all the way down the hall.

"Don't worry about me," answered the wolf. "Stay down!"

The kids ducked just as a new iteration of gunfire, this from Miranda or Luther's abandoned rifle, went plunging down the hall after them. Head whipping first, Paine scrambled around the corner and leapt beneath the basement steps just as the SWAT team burst through the stairwell's door.

"We've got you cornered, Garnet!"

One of the cops, rifle swinging first, came darting down the stairs and whipped around them to shine his flashlight.

His posture relaxed to see the kids cowering with their innocent stuffed dog.

"Clear," shouted the cop. "We've got some—"

Roger exchanged fire with whatever cops had already made it down the hall. The one who had discovered the children looked sharply toward the firefight.

"Stay down," he urged them. "Stay quiet."

While Miranda and Luther nodded, the cop dashed away.

As Luther emitted a long sigh of relief, Miranda yanked him up again. Paine followed after and soon they were once again upon the beast's back, the animal bounding up through the drop ceiling of the staff corridor and using claws to tear through the sheet rock beyond.

"Where are we going to go?" Luther's helpless question was directed to Paine, but Miranda took it upon herself to answer when inspiration struck.

"We can say we went to my parents' for lunch! Our house is nearby, they'll vouch for us. Let's say they sneaked us out to give us a bite to eat and we were there the whole time."

From the sounds of it, the cops were being chased back up the basement stairs and into the main floor by Roger's tenacious drive to get revenge on the kids who did this to him. While SWAT shouted orders to one another and exchanged fire with their target, Paine and the kids made their way back out to the roof of the school.

Miranda took a deep breath of fresh air for the first time in too long. The constant putrescence of death got to be a little too much for even her; and, as lacking in windows as the science museum was, the only way to escape it was to quite literally escape.

"Are you sure they'll help us? Really?"

"Sure, I'm sure."

While Paine thundered across the roof of the school and leapt smoothly to a nearby tree from whose branches he quickly bounced again, Miranda tightened her grip.

"Besides—I'm sure they'd love to meet both of you."

21

ROGER GARNET WAS going to get those psychopathic kids if it was the last thing he did.

It was why he had been put upon this earth.

He had always wondered. What purpose did he serve, drifting through this vast machine? And *what* a machine! The mushrooms revealed all its inner workings, layer by layer. Sometime around the encounter with Sheriff Hayward, the nauseating stomach full of mushrooms boosted his microdose into a full-blown trip that was, in spite of the horrors around him, somehow euphoric.

He had detached from this simian life—this quintessence of dust. Yes, ah! The phrase made perfect sense to him. He *was* dust—nothing more than dust,

dust that could choose at any time to collapse and leave this place.

Remember, man. Remember it was always only a choice, whether you knew it or not.

And, knowing it, Roger felt he would never be more ready than right now. This was the time—the ideal time!—for him to die.

But he could only die once his task was completed. Once the evil children who had done this had been eradicated.

All things had a place in existence, and even acts of criminal mass murder served a kind of symbolic purpose...but so did their punishment. There were those beings who existed to be heroes, or victims, or statistics, so that all the rest of the people in the world could live on and pass the torch of consciousness along the genetic line so appropriately called "the human race." And it *certainly* was a race. A relay.

Relay races had no room for a couple of selfish little psychopaths who would rather destroy the entire funrun than be a peaceful, productive part of it.

The mushrooms showed Roger the truth. He had grown them and consumed them at just the right time; this attack had happened at just the right time. Everything had happened at just the right time so this great trauma would serve its brutal purpose and then, upon its completion, be revenged like an infection culled once visible symptoms made more mysterious ones obvious.

Roger Garnet was a healer of humanity, and he would heal it by cutting away the infections. He had to be impassive about it; unemotional. He had therefore forced himself to kill Sheriff Hayward in a brutal way, in part because there was no coming back from a cop-killing but in part because he had never killed *anyone* before. The idea of starting with children, even when it was his civic duty, did not seem a simple matter by any stretch of the imagination.

But when they stood before him—with their demon, the wolf, the hideous anomaly that represented some kind of broken mechanism in the machine—suddenly, pulling the trigger became a simple thing.

Aiming was another story.

They almost got him. His head certainly hurt when he awoke, and he couldn't see quite as well anymore— but he could still see the tremendous shadow that was that hideous wolf, and the ghostly girl who seemed almost to invite his rifle fire.

So, Roger let the girl have it, or tried to. A hop, a skip, and a jump later, and, simply by virtue of it being his divine duty to carry out this cosmic revenge, Roger had managed to single-handedly force the semi-competent SWAT team back up the basement stairs to the main floor.

Though climbing the stairs made him dizzy, and he was pretty sure he had been shot by the cops at least once, (he wasn't sure—he couldn't feel anymore and had to consciously remember to keep holding the gun if he didn't want to forget it was in his hands and drop it), Roger's only stop was a quick regrouping in the shadow room. Panting in the dark, Roger backed around the corner of the room and was glad the cops didn't try to follow.

While he caught his breath, Roger braced himself against the wall and slid to the floor in the back corner.

He could not really *feel*, but it seemed as though the floor were oddly shaped—like he had taken a seat on a cushion full of rocks.

Standing to find he had left the floor soaked with blood that streamed from his headwound and along his spine, Roger used his rifle to poke open the duffel bag.

A flash illuminated the room and froze his shadow in motion.

A man with a gun, pointing to a bag of grenades.

While, outside, one of the police officers called for reinforcements, Roger pulled a pin and rolled one of the explosives out of the shadow room before ducking around the wall.

The cop gasped.

"Grena—"

Roger had already covered his ears, but he kept them covered another second or two because the ringing was so intense it seemed the explosion was still ongoing.

When the rattle of rubble falling to the floor reduced, Roger grabbed the gun and a few more grenades, pulled the pin on one of the latter, and lobbed it in the direction of the still shell-shocked officers while dashing to the back of the museum.

The cops shot after him belatedly; but, by the time they managed to take aim, the second grenade obliterated the concrete around them. While one screamed in agony, Roger pulled the next grenade and rolled it along behind him.

In the back of the main exhibit hall, Roger ducked through the staff door and ran down the blood-spattered hallway without pausing to lock or block anything. The back door was close enough that he didn't need to worry, and despite his head wound he remembered to touch his pocket to check for the spare set of keys still dripping with Hayward's gore.

Then, in the hallway, Roger pushed open the employee parking lot's east exit door and glanced outside through the crack.

More cops milled about—most of these, thankfully, in simple uniforms. There was no time to think or worry about what he was about to do.

After taking aim at the two SWAT members visible, Roger lobbed his last grenade. One, his gun already at attention for all the explosions ringing within the museum, took notice and cried out.

By jumping behind the bricked-in dumpsters, the cops just barely saved their own lives—and gave Roger a chance to look up as the wolf jumped from the roof of the science museum and across the treetops nearby.

Pale with divine rage, Roger raised his gun and released a war scream while firing into the regrouping cops. Officers in standard uniforms were the only ones hit, of course, the SWAT officers being preferential to showing bravado only when breaking into suspects' homes in the dead of night to look for drugs. This was a small town; hostage situations were entirely unheard of. Much as Hayward had suspected, they got into the force to be cool, not to save lives.

And that was why, with his brain exposed to the open air and left sometimes seeming like right, Bill Garnet still managed to make it to the van and take off after the wolf.

Even if he couldn't kill the kids, he at least had to get the monster that took Deborah's life. There was no question that it had killed before and would kill again—and, being an unearthly creature by all horrific appearances, it had no business killing in this world.

Honking wildly, Roger drove over curbs and across the lawn of the science museum to get on the road. A few cops, waving or shooting, chased after him several yards before charging for their cars. The lieutenant, in particular, seemed fiercely devoted to chasing him down, and was the first to plow after him with lights and sirens screaming.

He could not give up. he could not surrender. Roger Garnet would die woefully misunderstood however he finally died, but *he* would know—the universe would know—that he was doing the right thing by trying to murder these children and the demon posing as their imaginary friend.

Screeching onto the main road and hammering the gas, Roger wove in and out of traffic—and careened onto the sidewalk, when required—to get around drivers waiting for a green light. People screamed and leapt out of the way, or honked the horns of their own cars as though the problem were simply he did not see them or the police officers chasing after him; but, when he caught sight of the wolf running along the roof of the conjoined buildings of the nearby plaza, leaning out the window with the newly acquired AR-15 in his hand ended all question of road rage. Drivers rushed out of the way, colliding with one another in their attempts to make way for Roger. Moses, parting the Red Sea: he took aim at the wolf and earned a derisive glance from all three heads with his first, missed set of shots.

The gun leapt in his hand, braced but loosely against his shoulder and liable to fly away at any minute. Only adrenaline could keep him tolerating the recoil; only the reminder that it wouldn't matter kept him from thinking about the bruises.

While the assault rifle battered his shoulder with the next volley of shots and the wolf pulled off to leap through the downtown park, a pistol's crack drew Roger's attention.

Behind him, the lieutenant leaned out of the driver's side of his own vehicle and rectified his aim.

Roger slid back into the van and skidded around the parking circle of downtown's plaza. Without regard to the state of the van, he blasted out the other side to follow the busy streets of Smokeland along the length of the park which ran behind the businesses. He watched as closely as he could through his dark and blurry vision, swearing he sometimes caught a hint of movement in the trees.

As the movement transfigured into a wolf-like shadow that bounded across the buildings, over the street, and to the side where it could make its way toward residential neighborhoods, the van lurched. A quick consultation of the rear-view revealed the lieutenant's cop car smashing into the fender.

Gritting his teeth, Roger looked over his shoulder while guiding the unwieldy vehicle after the monster. The van seemed ready to tip, but it just managed to avoid total ruin and find its four tires on the ground again.

While he blasted through a red light, Roger leaned out and screamed at the lieutenant, "You're making a huge mistake!"

In response, the lieutenant fired off another round.

This time, he got the van's side mirror.

Roger yelped and leaned back into his seat, swerving to avoid a woman walking her dog before he once more mounted the curb to pass traffic.

He stepped on it, hoping to make it through the next green light and to the other side before he had competing traffic to cross.

Instead, he got one lane out before being t-boned by a car that, despite its small size, shot like a bullet into the side of the van and put an immediate halt to cosmic justice.

His ears ringing worse than after the grenades, Roger clutched his rifle. He couldn't let this stop him. He had to get the wolf. The door was stuck and he had to beat out the window and climb through the broken glass, but by God, Roger did it.

Outside, Harvey Carraway stumbled from his car with a sob and a look of terror for the cops. While the worried man ran off to continue his emergency trip to the museum (and his imperiled wife!) on-foot, Roger raised the gun weakly toward the increasingly distant wolf.

One last chance.

He pulled the trigger.

The AR-15, which had once belonged to Miranda, sputtered a few more rounds before coughing empty.

Swaying on his feet while the lieutenant and another pair of cops rushed up to place him under screaming arrest, Roger Garnet dropped the gun.

His only mission in life an abject failure, Roger looked the lieutenant helplessly in the eyes.

"Why'd you stop me?"

If the lieutenant made any response, Roger Garnet collapsed before he heard it.

22

LUTHER CLUNG TO his best friend for dear life, practically biting off his tongue to contain his screams. The wolf bounded from building to building to tree to building while, all the while, Miranda leaned around the boy to give directions.

"Let's head downtown," she shouted over the whipping wind of the wolf's hasty flight. "I'd prefer to lead them away from my family's house at first, if it's all the same to you."

"Good idea! Whoo boy, I hope they have a guest bed...I need a nap to sleep off all that food."

When Luther did force himself to open his eyes, it was only to check that the van from the science museum was making no headway. The by then familiar cracking and popping of gunfire reassured him that the police were attempting to take the situation in-hand...even if they weren't necessarily on the right side of things.

With all the bouncing he was doing on the back of the wolf, Luther couldn't decide if his nausea was motion sickness or shame.

Was he an evil person, or a victim? Both, somehow? He *had* finally shot someone and been complicit in the many other murders of the day...but hadn't he just been trying to survive?

Hadn't he?

Luther looked back over his shoulder, at the first person aside from himself who had ever actually seen Paine and lived. Miranda's dark eyes narrowed against the rushing air, and as her bob fluttered around her cheeks with her bow only slightly crooked from all the chaos, Luther thought to himself that she really would be a very beautiful lady someday.

The boy turned his eyes back to the fray when she noticed him staring, and he cried out with delight to find he'd glanced away just in time.

"Look!"

Miranda followed Luther's jutted finger and, for the first time that day, truly laughed. Amazing! Her bright witch's cackle competed with the crunch of metal on metal. While Roger Garnet's van was t-boned by a smaller car that nonetheless served to destroy both vehicles on impact, Miranda grasped

Luther's hand with a bright fire in her eyes.

"We're safe," she said, the sudden liveliness of her face somehow feral. Mad.

Yes—he really liked her.

"Um!"

Miranda's laughter was interrupted by Luther's stutter. While the wolf changed course at her tug of his fur, she waited for Luther to clear his throat.

"So, like, um, do you—want to hang out sometime?"

Her small mouth once again expanding into a somehow ill-suited smile, Miranda kissed his cheek.

While Luther leaned over the side of the wolf to finally puke with a combination of motion sickness and anxiety, Miranda laughed.

Reflexively tightening his grip on the wolf, Luther wiped his mouth. Guess that was a yes from both of them...better change the subject. Throat raspy for a few seconds, Luther glanced down at his friend.

"How come so many people have been able to see you today?"

"Oh," answered Paine amid his cheerful leaps and bounds, "that's easy! The only people who can see me are the people who are going to be killed by me."

"Oh," answered Luther and Miranda together, exchanging a look that was far more fearful in the boy than it was in the girl.

"*And* people I choose to show myself to, of course. Sheesh, don't worry."

Miranda hadn't been, but nobody liked a know-it-all. "You didn't kill Roger Garnet," she chose to more discreetly point out.

"Not yet," agreed the big beast. "Wowee! Swank neighborhood. Let me guess—yours is that big, black Victorian with all the crows sitting on it?"

"Ravens, actually."

"And my soul from out that shadow that lies floating on the floor shall be lifted," recited the wolf, his tone gay as he sprang toward the safety of the Even house, "Nevermore!"

AFTER

MIRANDA SLIPPED THE electrical tape from the lens of her webcam. She flicked a brisk glance into its black eye before sweeping her hands across the keys to answer Luther's video call.

"Hi, Miranda! Thanks, Mom." While Luther waved to his mother off-screen, then smiled toward Miranda, Miranda enjoyed the little flutter of batwings that constituted a slightly racing pulse. It happened sometimes when she saw Luther. She was worried she was suffering some kind of heart arrhythmia until the family witch doctor explained her frail human body was prone to things called emotions.

She later added him to her enemies list for over-explaining a basic concept to her.

"Did you have a good week, Miranda?"

"Yes, it was fun. My brother and I played hangman."

From off-screen, another voice: "I love that game! Who won?"

"I'm not sure I should say that on-camera. Hello, Paine."

When the wolf flopped into frame bearing a big doggie-grin, Luther settled against him without the least qualm. It was good to see their friendship had mended, although Miranda couldn't imagine Luther felt he had much choice.

"Miranda, Miranda. How are you, kiddo? How're your parents? Oh, what wonderful people!"

It perhaps should have come as no surprise to learn that Miranda's family had no trouble seeing Paine or being hospitable toward him, and no ethical qualm when it came to providing an alibi. Their respective school administrators were so relieved that the two unaccounted for children were not dead that neither got a reprimand for sneaking off to "have lunch at Miranda's house."

Like Miranda said...she just never got in real trouble.

"They said to send their love to you, Paine. They ask about you all the time."

"Shucks!"

As the wolf minced about, his paws upon his fuzzy cheeks as though to contain his blushing embarrassment, Luther rolled his eyes and elbowed the beast. "You just think her mom's pretty."

"And you don't?"

At Luther's cough, Miranda gently repressed the urge to kill her mother by reminding herself that it wasn't appropriate for a young lady to think those thoughts. Her responsibility to destroy Mrs. Even and take her place as the most powerful female of the bloodline was not yet due for many years, and she turned her attention away from the idea lest her mother sense it and get the upper-hand.

Luckily, Luther distracted her.

"Hey, um, speaking of parents, Miranda—mine were wondering, do you think that, next time we have a sleepover, we could have it at your house? My dad's had a nosebleed since the last time you slept in our guest room, and Mom wakes up crying at 4:44 every time you stay with us."

"No problem," said Miranda casually. "I'll have one of our in-law suites set up with a bed instead of a coffin. Do you still want to have the sleepover at the end of the month like usual, though?"

"Yeah!" The boy nodded eagerly, clearly finding it as important to keep in close contact as she did. With the children separated by a drive of two hours, their only opportunities to visit were self-made. Miranda jotted a little note on her desk calendar as Luther continued, "I'm sure excited to come over and hang out."

With a glance that caused the wolf to scurry up and obligingly shut the door to their bedroom, Luther leaned toward the camera.

"Plus," he said softly, "my parents are always watching the news these days."

"You need to find a show to be interested in, or a video game, so you can maintain control of the television. They don't need to be watching that drivel."

"I don't think they're going to figure anything out, but it makes me nervous. What if he—"

"Don't even think about it." Settling back in her computer chair with her pencil poised between the thumbs and indexes of both hands, Miranda stared Luther down through the screen. "If something happens, we'll fix it. But for now, Luther...why don't we just focus on being kids?"

His nostrils expanding in a huffed exhalation, Luther nodded.

"You're right. Oh! Did I tell you about this card tournament—"

Like many feminine counterparts, Miranda politely nodded and 'Mmhm'ed her way through a dull subject for the sake of her boyfriend.

The truth was that her attempt to protect Luther's innocence was one-sided. She did not care about herself. She had never been innocent and had no interest in preserving anything that did not serve her.

In fact, outside of maintaining her friendship with Luther and Paine, Miranda had only one real interest these days.

After talking for forty minutes, until being cut off by Mr. and Mrs. Watson, Miranda said good-night to

Luther and shut down the video call software.

She replaced the tape on her camera, turned off her computer, and leaned back in her seat.

Her eye was caught by the pinboard behind the monitor, where the headline that sometimes appeared in her sleep blazed furious black and white.

SHOOTING SUSPECT COMATOSE AFTER CAR CHASE

There were a bevy of other articles, photographs, schedules and database print-outs held by pins and twine, but that initial Sunday morning article was always where her eye landed first.

After regarding it and its accompanying staff photo of Roger Garnet at a science museum event from the prior year, Miranda realized she was swinging her desk chair back and forth.

Her lips pursed.

Annoyed to have caught herself in a useless nervous habit, Miranda slid a binder out of her desk, cracked open the cover labeled *SAINT JOHN'S HOSPITAL EMPLOYEE HANDBOOK*, and commenced her nightly study of the hospital maps.

OTHER PAPERBACK WORKS
FROM PAINTED BLIND PUBLISHING

REGINA WATTS

INDUSTRIAL DIVINITY (2020)

WILD GIRL RUNNING (2020)

DOTTIE FOR YOU SEASON 1 (2021)

THE BURNINGSOUL SAGA (2021-2022)

I WAS AN OP DEMON LORD (2021-2022)

BE MY BULLY (2021)

SEDUCED BY SABINE (2021)

M. F. SULLIVAN

DELILAH, MY WOMAN (2015)

THE LIGHTNING STENOGRAPHY DEVICE (2017)

THE DISGRACED MARTYR TRILOGY (2019-2020)

www.ingramcontent.com/pod-product-compliance
Lightning Source LLC
Chambersburg PA
CBHW021310190726
48288CB00003B/782